W9-AEA-705

LONG RIDE TO NOWHERE

Center Point
Large Print

This Large Print Book carries the
Seal of Approval of N.A.V.H.

LONG RIDE TO NOWHERE

William A. Luckey

CENTER POINT PUBLISHING
THORNDIKE, MAINE

R
CASS COUNTY PUBLIC LIBRARY
400 E. MECHANIC
HARRISONVILLE, MO 64701

0 0022 0329774 8

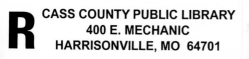

This Center Point Large Print edition
is published in the year 2008 by arrangement with
Golden West Literary Agency.

Copyright © 1987 by William A. Luckey.

All rights reserved.

The text of this Large Print edition is unabridged. In other
aspects, this book may vary from the original edition.
Printed in the United States of America.
Set in 16-point Times New Roman type.

ISBN: 978-1-60285-150-4

Library of Congress Cataloging-in-Publication Data

Luckey, William A.
Long ride to nowhere / William A. Luckey.--Center Point large print ed.
p. cm.
ISBN 978-1-60285-150-4 (lib. bdg. : alk. paper)
1. Large type books. I. Title.

PS3612.U265L66 2008
813'.6--dc22

2007043543

To Kate, Rob, and Bill

Preface

This book is fiction; names and incidents are the product of the writer's imagination. However, some of the occurrences revolve around the history of the times, and the city of Tucson in the Territory of Arizona.

General George Crook was stationed in the territory from September 1882 to April 1886 with express orders to bring a solution to the escalating Apache problem, and Geronimo in particular. Crook chased and finally met with Geronimo, and convinced the Indian leader to bring his people back across the American border to the reservation. At the last moment, a whiskey peddler, some say a man in the service of the infamous and undocumented 'Tucson Ring,' fed whiskey to the Indians and convinced them the soldiers would slaughter them all if they crossed the border. The Indians fled back into the wilderness. Crook was replaced in early April of 1886 by General Nelson A. Miles, and, after seeing some seventy-five peaceful Indians shipped back east by train, left the Tucson area.

George Crook was an independent soldier. Usually dressed in a flat straw hat and canvas jacket and pants, and riding a mule, he was often taken for anything but the commanding officer. At one point, he was offered a job skinning mules for his own company by a man who had not yet met his employer. Crook rarely took advantage of the comforts given an officer in the field but chose to eat and camp in the same manner as his men. His presence in the desert south of the San Pedro river at the time of this book is quite possible.

William A. Luckey

★ Chapter 1

"So, Marshal. What have you got in your fine hotel for me this morning."

The soft voice intruded into the morning chill of the small office. Lambert Dawson allowed the smallest of smiles to break his before coffee sulks. His hand stopped in midair and he turned around very slowly, allowing a grin to build inside him.

The smile widened to put a gleam in the dull hazel eyes, set close in the long face. "What makes you think I got anyone locked up in this establishment simple enough to head out with you this trip? Word's out, mister. All I got is a two-bit horse thief, a drunk, and a hoorawing cowhand." Dawson paused for effect, letting a puzzled look contort his face. "Come to think on it, any one of them's good enough to ride for you."

The two men watched each other; the lawman's long body bent deeper in its stoop to search the face of the smaller man. His visitor stood just inside the office door. Below average height, he was dwarfed by the height of his friend. The man was leaning against the frame of the door, his hands and face stained a walnut brown by sun and heritage, his strong jaw softened by the graying fringe of a beard. His dark eyes glittered as he worked over the people offered by his friend. There was a difference to the man beyond his darkness: a line of color down the hard woolen pants, an extra width to the hat brim touching his thigh, a belt hammered of etched silver discs.

"Ah, yes. The Señor Maldinado, it is my greatest pleasure," the marshal said as he leaned over in a grand, sweeping gesture to bring the smaller man inside. His reward was a wide grin as the man passed his bowed head and went directly to the small stove and hissing pot. There was no jingle to his steps; his feet were cradled in soft half-boots unadorned with roweled spur or fancy inlay.

Rafael Maldinado poured the two cups of coffee, taking a moment to blow out the dried bug inside one cup. Lambert Dawson took the offering and grinned at his compadre. They went back a long time together. The cups were raised in silent salute. Then both men took their first sip, and winced at the scalding bitter burn. Two sighs came in unison, and they chuckled, the sound growing louder at the pleasure of the moment. It was Dawson who spoke first.

"Heard you was out to the Figured S this time, did some good trading. Word out you brought enough men this time, planning on taking the herd back tomorrow. So's I heard. Got enough beef to feed an army."

Rafael nodded. "Indeed that is what we are doing. We are chasing the Indians again, the cavalry has come in to settle them, and so we must feed them. I must return quickly to my family."

They settled into an easy silence. The visitor raised his eyes above the steaming cup, smiled at the usually talkative marshal, and tilted his head in question. Dawson grinned and continued his ramblings.

"Ole George Ryder, he says you finally got him to part with that fancy mare you been wanting. And she just dropped herself a fine he-colt. What you need with another high-blooded bronc makes no sense to me." He sighed dramatically. "But then, I never did learn to figure you out."

"Yes, my old friend, I have gotten the mare. And the colt is a special one. So now I have need of one more man. But it does not sound like your hotel is holding what I am looking for. The mare must be walked to my ranch very slowly, and she and her babe must have the care of a good man. I can only come to you and ask, and hope. You are the one who knows these men."

Lambert Dawson tugged at an ear and looked down to smile at his longtime friend. They had lived in each other's lives for a brief time and had never forgotten the bond. He started to speak, hesitated, and coughed harshly, then spat at the dulled spittoon in the corner. This time he was not sure.

"Just maybe I got what you need. Kid been hanging around here 'bout eight, nine months. Good hand with a rope, better with gentling the broncs. Got more work than he can handle proper. Ought to see him talk a white-eyed snorting son into standing still for a lady to ride. A sight for damned sure.

You say the mare needs to be walked back real slow, a long lonesome ride. Be a good place for this one. Been in more brawls than any one man got a right to. Come Saturday night and I got to go looking for him to pick him up 'fore the others do. Don't seem to start nothing, but he sure enough is in the middle."

The distress in his friend was easy for Maldinado to recognize. "Why do you think, with this unholy recommendation, that he would do the work for me?"

Lambert shook his long head slowly. "Don't rightly know. Hell of a look to him, makes you want to plant a fist in his nose. But he ain't dishonest and . . . I don't rightly know.

"Anyway, he got himself fired this past week, right out of the Figured S. Stayed working there the longest. Hit town and took a swing at one of the Figured S riders. Then turned on my deputy, broke two 'a Bob's ribs. Took a pistol barrel to settle him."

Dawson shook his head at the memory. "So he's setting right here, waiting for you and living in the last cell. A few more days and he'll get to calling it home. You want a looksee, go right ahead. Ain't got to writing the charges on him yet. Been waiting for you."

A most peculiar recommendation. Not a kind word or good thought, yet Dawson still wanted him to see the kid. Rafael nodded his understanding, and went past his friend to the locked door leading to the narrow line of cells.

The smell of coffee had brought him partially awake, and then the surprising sound of laughter had brought him upright on the hard edge of the bunk. Damn the law for locking up a man for defending himself. He rubbed at the black-and-blue welt above his eye, and winced at the result. Then Blue Mitchell raised his long arms up over his head, clenching his bony hands together in a tight squeeze, pulling against the tightness in his shoulders. The long muscles down his neck and across his back spasmed from the pull, and his lean face twisted in a grimace.

It took him a long time to sit up, to unfold his length of leg and body carefully, to swing over the edge of the cot provided with such care by the law of Beaufort, Utah. Blue rested his head in the comforting nest of his hands, blocking out the spreading light that came from the one high window behind him. Winter-darkened blond hair flowed past his eyes to cover most of his face. He leaned harder into his hands, elbows digging deeply into the corded muscle just above each knee. Damn these hard nights and cold mornings. Damn this whole entire damnable town.

It could have worked here. He was older now, no longer a scrawny kid too easy to pick on, too weak to fight back. Blue snorted through his hands. He had a skill to offer with these hands now, but skills weren't enough. He hadn't learned how to get along with folks yet, how to talk easy and back away without losing himself. But he was always being pushed, men turning their anger at missed throws and lost loves on him.

Goddamn.

Footsteps brought his head up; not the law's this time, not Lambert Dawson's heavy and too-familiar tread. Softer steps, lighter, with a steady cadence that came quickly to his end cell and stopped.

Blue looked up at the intruder and met a pair of dark

eyes that did not give way under his stare. He took his own steady measure of this man: compact, dark, certain of himself. Money, too, by the looks of his gear. Soft cream shirt, still clean; silk kerchief knotted in a bright splash of red; fine leather vest; and the give-away of the silver belt and thin braid. Didn't see too many like this one; sure was out of his territory.

The level eyes stayed on him, probing him, looking deep into him, but without the too-familiar flush of growing anger. The length of time and the knowing dark eyes made Blue conscious of the dirt imbedded in his knuckles, the frayed and collarless shirt stained dark under each arm, the mended tear down the outside of his faded jeans. His own smell offended him. He rubbed at the welt again, then cursed softly. It was an effort not to look away from the dark face. A heat rose in him, be damned the man.

Blue Mitchell rose slowly, never letting his eyes wander from the man just beyond the narrow, barred door. The dark head came up as Blue unfolded, the dark eyes went quickly up and down his six-foot length. Blue knew the man had him now. He shook his head, strings of wild hair slapping against his face.

Rafael knew why Lambert Dawson had this man as a guest every week in his fine jail. And he could guess at the talent that lay in those limber hands, that loose-jointed body. Despite the easy grin that came and stayed on the wide mouth, despite the obvious youth of the lean body, the awkwardness to the long arms and legs, there was a ready look of insolence to the face that would breed its own trouble.

It was the eyes. Heavy-lidded eyes set deep in the narrow face. A homely face that hollowed out beneath flattened cheekbones. A face made younger by the almost white blond stubble of a thin growth of beard, framed with the flow of blond hair, matted and hanging below where there should have been a collar.

It was the eyes: a dark green-blue framed by black lashing, outlined by a startling contrast of white. They carried a natural insolence that would constantly keep the owner in trouble. And yet there was something in this wild-looking young man that Lambert Dawson wanted him to have. Rafael kept his silence and watched the impatience come to a head.

"You seen enough yet . . . Mister?" There was a wait before the title, a moment long enough to draw insult, to bring a flush of anger. The voice matched the eyes, soft, polite, with a cocky slurring that drew blood. Rafael only smiled and continued to watch. The deep blueness of the eyes flushed a darker green as anger built up in the prisoner. Rafael deliberately added to the fire.

"You are not where you can challenge another, my friend. You are at my mercy. So why not listen to what I am to offer and then speak your mind to me. You cannot lose anything but time."

Blue shrugged his shoulders and turned away. Another one who wanted to ride him, break him to bit and spur. Just like that damned long-headed marshal. One stride brought him to the half-full tin bucket, its odor ripening in the beginnings of the new day's warmth. One more step brought him to the coldness of the high-stacked rock wall, the sill of the narrow window that brightened the air just above him. There was silence from the man behind him.

That son of a bitch was right. Blue turned around slowly on one boot heel, and looked back at the man, who waited with great patience on the other side of the barred door.

"What you want with me? Dawson's got to let me out soon enough. I ain't looking for nothing from you."

He caught the escaping rage in his voice and steadied the last few words. The cell grew smaller, the thin metal bars leaned in on him, threatened to touch his back, push at his side. Then the dark faced man spoke his words with a soft knowing.

"But I am looking for something from you. I need a man to take a mare to my ranch. To walk with her and her new foal. A man who knows enough of horses, who will travel slowly and take great care. For this Señor Dawson says you are the man. And I believe him. For this only he is willing to let you go free. And soon."

Blue couldn't stop his snort of disbelief. Dawson had no cause to do any favors for him, to believe in him. Believe in what? His ability to fight? The words continued from the man, and Blue set his mind not to listen. But the voice was soft, and persuasive.

"I will pay your fine out of here, provide you with a

good horse and a pack mule, and will pay you well the day you ride into my ranch. For this only will the marshal let you go so soon. Otherwise . . ."

Blue thought it over. A nursemaid. Must be some piece of horseflesh to be worth the effort of an extra hand. And this man must be in his own hurry or he would be making the ride himself.

It could be another start. The fresh one he thought his town held for him. A long ride alone to a new land where some didn't even speak his own brand of language. A chance for him to get out of this town, this whole damned state. He'd had enough fights here to last a goodly while.

Before he nodded his acceptance, the dark rancher put his hand through the bars. The tapered fingers were clean, the nails trimmed, but there was a buildup of callused padding at the base of each finger and across the palm. This was a working boss.

"I am glad you will be riding with the mare." The small hand disappeared in Blue's long one, the dark skin a contrast to the reddened and cracked knuckles, the faded yellow coloring of last summer's sun. But the strength in the hands was equal.

"I am Señor Rafael Maldinado. And you are called?"

"Blue. Blue Mitchell."

"Ahhh." The word was drawn out to a long sigh. And the dark eyes went over him one more time. Finally, they came to rest on the homely face, holding the gaze of the strange sea-blue eyes.

"Yes, you are the right one."

The señor was gone before Blue got to his own ques
tioning. He watched the set to the back, the eas
horseman's walk, as the man disappeared through th
door to the office. Then Blue took the one step tha
brought him to the tin bucket to relieve himself. Th
slow grin stuck to his face. He was on his way out o
here.

Lambert Dawson was a fair man, as the law went. S
it seemed to Blue. Breakfast always arrived before th
town got to moving on its own. The board that serve
for a bed these past four days would now become hi
table. Blue was hungry. He was always hungry.

His grin widened. From the shape of this morning h
would be out of here soon, and with the pocket jingl
to buy his own meals. But he still wanted his mornin
grub. A growing boy needed his eats. And by his reck
oning, his birthday was coming up in the next fe
days. Might even be close to twenty-one by now
never would know for certain. His age changed ofte
when he was a boy, depending on how useful it coul
be. But he knew the date. April 9. That was one certai
thing he did know.

★ Chapter 2

Blue was careful. Two steps out the door and the su
hit his eyes, took away his sight, and blinded him t
the tipping of the walkway. He stopped then, an
waited until his eyes adjusted themselves to the noo
sun. The cold was still there, coming down from th

now-peaked mountains, but the sun was reaching for eight now, and he had been locked up for four long lays. He blinked twice more, and stood, watching the lmost-deserted street.

The voice came from right behind him, and Blue lamped down on the impulse to spin around, his hand utomatically reaching for the pistol not yet back on is hip. He thought he'd left the law back in the small eated office. But Lambert Dawson wasn't letting him et away that easy.

"There's a horse for you, down to Pat's livery. Talked to Pat and he'll give you a horse with no rouble, if you don't mouth off. He's had enough of ou, like the rest of us. The Señor'll be waiting out to he Figured S. You hear this boy. By God, you better e to the ranch 'afore supper, or the whole town'll be ut as a posse after you. You hear me?"

Blue liked the anger rising in the law's slow voice. He turned his head just enough to see the sorrowful ace of his jailor.

"I hear you, Marshal. You worried I won't get out of our town fast enough. Not much can happen from ere to the livery, and there you got Pat on his best ehavior. I'll be out and gone soon enough. You bet."

"You watch it with Pat, boy. He never forgive you or the paint mare you sold him lady broke. Damned ear to kill him. So watch yourself and get a move on."

Blue only shook his head and walked carefully to the dge of the walk, then turned one more time to grin at he law before stepping off into the muddy street.

Dawson watched the long figure amble crossways to the shabby livery barn. He shook his head in despair as a rider had to swerve to avoid running the boy down. Trouble even walking across a goddamn street. He waited several long minutes, then sighed with relief as he recognized the swaying body on the high-headed bronc coming out of the wide-open livery door. Guess Pat had eased up on his temper for this last meeting.

He sure hoped to hell his judgment of the kid wasn't wrong, that was something to him. Hell, even the town curs took to following the youngster on his Saturday night lonesomes. He was hoping Rafael could rope in the wildness, turn it to something good on that ranch of his way down there in the desert. Dawson shook his head mournfully one more time. Sure hoped the kid worked out.

The livery horse wasn't worth stealing, but the idea picked at Blue's mind. The animal fought every stride, pitching and pulling to run. His meager gear had already been tied to the back of his old hull, waiting only for his appearance to be tossed over the back of the rank grullo. Not worth stealing, but he'd be damned if he'd do anything more than cut the horse loose and let it run. His head ached and he wiped at the blood crusting in the corner of his mouth. Pat had gotten in his last few licks. He should have known better than to trust the lawman's word.

The sun felt good, the air smelled clean, even the roll and pitch of the eager horse was a relief, loosening his nuscles, clearing his head. Blue pulled his hat free and lapped the bronc on the shoulder as he dug in his ieels. The grullo bellied down and bolted the quiet treet, leaving scattered streaks of mud and surprised aces as a final salute to Beaufort, Utah from Blue Aitchell.

Rafael was impatient to head out, to get back home before much longer. The cattle were road-branded and eady. They were heading out now, and he, too, would eave today, trusting the high-headed brown gelding he ode to take him hard and fast to the mountains just to he east of the city of Tucson. Rafael's nerves kept his iand too tight on the bridle, and the brown spun in a ight circle against the unaccustomed stinging in his nouth. The Indians were off the San Carlo reservation. t was time for him to ride home.

He let the brown gelding run and brought the horse n a wide circle back down the sloping hill to the Figured S headquarters. There was a horse coming fast, on the north road that led to the town of Beaufort. The brown slid from his run to a smooth stop, settled and tood quietly. Rafael crossed his hands on the low horn of the saddle, leaning on the heavy swell.

His dark eyes narrowed as he watched the wild run of the livery bronc, and he swore softly to himself as he grullo slid into the yard, front legs high, mouth vide. The boy was down and at the cinch before the iorse was on four legs. Two quick tugs at the old hull, a pull at the slip eared bridle, and the grullo was free.

Before Rafael could speak up, the rider slapped th bronc's shoulder with the sweated blanket. The grull kicked out at the wavering shadow, then found hi freedom and fled from the corrals, headed out to th open grass.

"That was not your horse to turn loose." The lon body of the boy twitched slightly at the words, but th sullen face gave no more acknowledgment than tha small gesture. Rafael pushed the brown gelding close to the high shouldered rider, and spoke again.

"That was not your horse to free."

Blue swung around fast, spooking the brown sending the fine head back into the rider's hands.

"You can take that crowbait out of my pay. Then he' mine to set free."

There was a sharpness to the words that brough Rafael one step closer to look at his new hand. Ther was a fresh cut at the corner of the wide mouth, spreading bruise across the cracked knuckles of th right hand, and a wildness to the vivid eyes that told it own story. But Blue Mitchell said nothing more, onl stood with feet planted wide apart, patched gear in on hand, watching the new boss. Rafael sighed and let i go.

"I will show you the mare. And her colt. Come wit me, and we will settle you with your supplies and will show you the map that takes you to my ranch. Yo must not hurry on this ride, but you will travel stead Give the colt a chance to toughen up, but with muc care. And much thought for your charges."

Blue dropped the gear against the barn wall and will-ngly settled into stride alongside the smaller man. He vas puzzled; the challenge had not been taken. It had ot been ignored, or hidden, but put aside as if unim-ortant. Guess he now owned a grullo mustang run-ing somewhere in the plains beyond Beaufort. He rinned; this was not a man to bristle and strut like a arnyard bully. Blue glanced down at the man who vas his boss. He walked one stride ahead of Blue, alking in that soft and insistent voice, telling him of he breeding of this fine mare, of the perils of the long rip into his country. It was easy to hear the words and et them wash away the residue of anger. Blue quick-ned his stride to keep pace as they came to the corral.

She truly was a fine mare. About 15 hands, good hested, a rich seal brown with heavy dapples showing hrough her rough-shed winter coat. A strip of white isected the clean head, wider at the large eyes, apering and ending in a diamond above the thin flare f nostrils. Hard legs, short bone, clean and tight with good forearm and sloping shoulder. The foal was a right chestnut, clean-headed like his dam, but already arrying the hint of size and breadth she lacked.

Blue stopped inside the pen gate, then slid down the ost at his back slowly, making no move that would pook the colt or worry the mare. He forgot about the ays in jail, the dark weal spreading across his temple, he foul words and the sting of the quirt that had ended is dealings at the livery. That was all behind him.

Soft sounds came from his throat, muttered

soothing sounds that brought the tiny ears of the foal to stand straight. The mare slowed her chewing of the fine timothy hay, and stood quietly, one errant strand of the faded green grass hanging from her soft lips. Blue stayed on his heels. Slowly, one hand came up from his thigh to turn palm up, fingers wiggling slightly. He did not notice the Señor walk away from the fence to stand inside the barn. He did not see the riders come in from the long fence line. He sang softly, mindlessly, head down and eyes half-closed, demanding nothing and waiting for the shy colt to take the first step.

Tiny lips touched his long fingers and then moved away. Blue remained still. The mare took one step and whickered softly; the foal swung his head and came back to the enticement of the moving fingertips. His short, red neck stretched out; his warm breath touched Blue's face.

Then Blue felt the heavier weight of the mare's step, could sense her standing over him. Head still lowered, eyes averted, he sang his quiet words, hand palm-up, asking for nothing. Then the mare dropped her muzzle to his blond hair and picked at a strand. She tugged and then chewed reflectively, finally dropping the tasteless morsel and pushing against his face. Blue laughed gently, and stroked the flat jowl of the mare. Then he reached beyond her to the soft fuzz of the baby's forelock. Both animals stood near his hunched body and he stayed with them, head down and quiet, humming tunelessly.

"God damn it, what the hell you think you're doing, who the hell are you?"

The loud voice spun the mare away from Blue. The colt staggered backward in panic, and Blue fought the impulse to roar to his feet at the hated familiarity of the sound. He waited until the mare and colt fled to the far side of the pen and stopped their circling. The foal buried his face in the mare's flank, butting at her udder, desperate for supper.

That freed him. He whirled and ducked through the gate and without stopping landed head first in the belly of Bristol Adderson. He knew that voice, the loud bullying tone that had made his days a misery on this sorry ranch for too long. Adderson stumbled under the attack, heels digging frantically to find purchase in the soft dirt, arms windmilling for balance.

The rush of weight carried them both to the ground. Adderson was a confirmed brawler; he immediately rolled on his foe, hugging Blue and winding his stubby arms around the lean chest, butting his head at those hated blue eyes he could just see. Blue jammed a knee into Bristol's crotch, but the man twisted easily and took the blow on one large thigh. The round head caught the blackening weal on Blue's temple, sending a shock that stunned. Adderson kept his advantage, and rolled over again to pin the lighter man under him. One big hand found the corded throat, one fist pulled back for a pounding blow.

Blue could do nothing. Pinned by the extra fifty pounds, stunned by the crack on his head, he pried his eyes open to watch the fist grow smaller, then bigge He closed his eyes again and tried for one last buck t move the mountain sitting on him.

Then strong fingers circled Bristol's wrist, whil other fingers dug into his shoulder, finding nerves tha pinched and bit hard. A soft voice gave him no choice

"You will get up, Mr. Adderson. You will leave thi man alone. I know you ride for the Figured S, but yo will not fight with this man."

Bristol loosened his hand wrapped around the muscled nuck, pushed away from the body beneath him i an awkward motion, and stood up, swaying slightly body tingling from the unused anger riding him. H looked down at Blue's long form at his feet, please with the blood trickling from the mouth, and th swelling bruise on the forehead. Then those hated blu eyes looked back at him, and the goddamn son of bitch grinned.

Bristol looked to the man who had given him th command, hoping for a second chance.

"You sure you know what you're doing with thi one? He'll take whatever you got and more. Wouldn' let him near that mare if I was you."

He shook his head in unreasoning anger. "You th boss, you want this sorry son, you got him."

With that final word, Bristol walked away, still trembling with the energy of the unfinished fight. Had th son this time, too, but Bristol knew when he wa licked. If he was riding with the Señor's herd, it wa no time to fight with the dumb-eyed bastard. Ther vas always later. Someday he'd get that son alone.

The toe of a soft boot dug gently at Blue's ribs. He ooked up into the face of the Señor. Blue's grin videned. A hand came down to him, offering help. 'he shock of the gesture came and went quickly .cross Blue's long face, but Rafael Maldinado saw it .nd wondered that one so young would have so little aith. Then the long fingers found his and Rafael set imself to pulling hard against the weight of the lowned man. But Blue Mitchell rose quickly, barely ieeding the help to stand on his own.

A hand on his shoulder turned Blue to face his boss. 'You did not need to fight that man. A word from me .nd there would be no fight. Why then did you choose o?"

"That there son of . . . Adderson, he's been at me ince I come in. Worked for Bryer for a long while on his ranch. Adderson always was looking to tell me vhat to do, reason I quit here. Don't take those words rom no man."

"So, my young friend. You have the responsibility iow to take this fine mare and her foal on a long ourney. Are you going to fight each man who quesions you? Are you going to brawl your way south, or vill you care for your charges and hold your temper? cannot afford to lose this mare through your imagned insults. This time you must make a choice."

Blue opened his mouth to protest, then saw there vas nothing he could offer beyond his temper and his eputation. Knowing all about him, this dark man was still offering to take the risk, willing to trust him an his judgment. Knowing that put a different set t Blue's temper.

He looked for Adderson, and saw him across th ranch yard, stooped over the water trough, splashing a the dirt and blood. Blue brought his gaze back to th older man who was watching him with such intensity It was a tough choice.

Several long strides brought him near the man Adderson straightened up quickly and one hand wen to a pistol newly-belted to his thick waist. He spat ou the words from bruised lips.

"What you want, boy? I been warned off by the bos so you best leave this. Or do you like your fighting thi easy?"

Blue said nothing, only watched the round face o the heavyset puncher settle into its accustomed sou lines. He dipped his head to shadow his eyes and pu out his right hand.

"Sorry, Bristol. You was looking out for your job."

Adderson stared at the hand almost as if to count th fingers, to check for the hidden trick. He looked u into Blue's face, found no heat in the odd blue eyes and then took the proffered hand. The two men shook slowly, hands going up and down twice. Then they broke apart and Adderson went back to his washing Nothing was changed; someday he would get this on all to himself and finish the fight. Adderson's hatre went deep.

Blue looked for Maldinado. He saw only quic

novement as the man stepped into the big barn that Bryer had let him use for his stock. Inside, Blue found him smoothing a double folded blanket over the back of a deep gold buckskin. Blue's rough saddle straddled the wooden stall divider. Without looking up, the Señor spoke.

"You will be ready to ride in the hour. This it Tico. He will go quietly with you and the mare, and not bother about the colt. There is a mule packed and ready. I have papers for you, detailing your journey, proving your right to have the mare. There are clothes, fresh bought. It is time for you to ride. There is fifty dollars waiting for you, plus a horse of your choice. And I will pay for the grullo you set free. A deal?"

Blue heard the words and watched the dark face. Rafael Maldinado continued to smooth out the woolen pad, stroking the shiny neck of the patient gelding. There were words that had not yet been spoken, and they had to be said.

"The fifty dollars and a fine horse are worth far more to you than the fleeting ownership of the dark mare and her son. Keeping them can only give you much grief."

It was done. Blue smiled. No bluster, no pictures of blood or promise of pain, just the simple words. He nodded his understanding and smiled.

"Be getting my gear, want to go over them directions with you. Don't want to be getting lost just the other side of the ridge. Pretty damned shameful."

★ Chapter 3

Three days it took before they got it sorted out. Thre long and slow days. The mare tugged and pulled at th lead rope almost to the point of wearing it out. Th first day's distance wasn't more than two miles, an the chestnut colt was the reason. Blue had figured o only a few miles anyway, knowing the youngste would tire fast and become footsore. By the secon day he was wishing this was true; the colt ran an dodged shadows, kicking out at the slow-movin buckskin. The son was enjoying his new freedom, nc knowing there was a direction and a purpose to th small group's traveling. The mare lengthened Blue' arm a good two inches by her pulling, and numbed hi ears with her screams.

The mule settled the situation. The big colt trie nursing on the deliberate animal, and received a well aimed kick that sent the baby sideways squalling i pain and fear. The mare spun around at the sound, hal pulling Blue from the saddle. It took another hour fo the mare to settle and the colt to finish lunch. Blue dis mounted and tied the buckskin and the mule to stubby tree. He figured to lean back and enjoy smoke, then try for another mile.

He was too slow in knowing the colt was done. B the time Blue untangled the mule from the buckskin' tail and gathered the reluctant mare, the colt was dow flat and out in the short grass. He swore softly unde is breath and climbed one more time down from the uckskin's back. This trip was going to take forever.

He couldn't help but laugh. He had nothing much ut forever right now. Riding another man's horse, sing another man's gear, even wearing his store-ought clothes. What he did own for himself weren't uch for bragging on; a battered saddle, two clean and atched shirts, a blanket-lined coat, and a pair of oots. The rest was the Señor's.

It was looking up, seemed to him. In another month e'd have the papers on a good horse and hard cash in is pocket, more than he'd ever seen that belonged to im. Blue nodded his head once in hard satisfaction. ould be a time for decisions, time for another new eginning. It was up to him; today was his birthday nd it was his choice. He decided he was twenty-one ow, age as good as any, and the fifty dollars was his rst birthday present. To himself.

lue spent a lot of time sitting under that stubby tree, oing over the map, checking the thin penciled line of ails, nodding his understanding at the marks in the argins: places to avoid, ranches that were safe, towns at were questionable. Nice that the man assumed he ould read. He could, barely, follow the directions, iven a lot of time to puzzle them out. He'd learned to ad from an 'aunt' who gave him the basics.

An uncle had hired him out to another rancher when e was probably 12 years old and lying to be 14. The ife inlcuded him with her own brood for schooling, said he kept her ten-year-old in line. He'd stayed a that spread for three years, and then the schoolin stopped when the lady died in childbirth delivering he eighth baby. One more year and Blue had it out wit the rancher, taking a beating over the danged kid th dogged his trail.

That had been his last year as a boy. He was tall fo his age and he grew the hard way, earning his wage on a big spread running for the cookie, pulling all th dirty chores. But he wasn't hired out by his great uncl anymore. From that time on he kept his wages and wa smart enough to ride out of the small Wyoming valle The old man vowed to chase him down for the cash said it was due him as the boy's kin.

Blue shuddered at the memories, feeling cold in th high spring warmth. Damn. He best not sit here an wander in the past. He rose unsteadily from the base c the tree, and slapped the dozing buckskin hard on th butt. The even-tempered horse opened one eye and pu his weight back on both hind legs, getting ready t move out. Blue swore out loud this time, hands o hips, head tilted back. He let loose with all he kne and more he made up. Took near to ten minutes, but h felt a lifting of the old memories and a cleanness i him. Damn, he wasn't never going back to thos thoughts again. Ahead was a whole new life. And th trail he was riding was clear as far as he could see.

One week out, and Blue had enough of the clear sk and wide grass lands. They went on forever. There wa nough grub and fixings that he had no need to stop at town or ranch looking for something special. The eñor had seen to that. And Blue was planning on aking his instructions seriously. When he heard men iding nearby or saw dust coming up behind him, he ulled aside into the brush to let the riders pass, to eep himself and his stock unnoticed. But he sure vould have liked to hear a voice other than his own.

The slow, easy walk to the buckskin did him in. Put im half asleep on the wide comfort of the horse's ack. Easy enough to slip the reins over the horn, fold is hands, and let the warm sun give him a rest. He odded, head touching lightly on his chest, body going vith the four-beat motion of the monotonous walk.

The mule jerked sideways, the contrary mare pulled ack, and the buckskin stopped. Blue's hand went to is pistol, which came out easily from the oiled holter. He raised himself in the saddle, swung around in half circle to each side, gun following his eyes, ooking for something. There was nothing in sight but nore grass and swelling hills.

As he settled back, habit made him check the stock. The mare was resting easy, the colt quick to nurse with greedy pulls. It was the mule. Blue looked at the nouse-colored animal and swore. Somebody done ome bragging once about these critters being sureooted, and there the damned fool animal stood, one ind foot balancing on a rock. Blue tugged on the lead, ut the mule refused to move.

He walked behind the buckskin, cautious as he got to

the mule. The big head swung at him, the ears flopping madly, but the beast did not shift his weight or prepare his hind end for his normal challenging kick. Some-thing must have caught a hoof. Blue slipped out his knife, and sure enough, when he stooped down for a closer look, he found the trouble.

The damnedest thing. The hind shoe had caught the edge of a flat bit of rock; the mule must have taken one step with the rock trapped there. When his weigh came down on the stone, the mule stopped. But tha one step had twisted the shoe. Blue jimmied his knife blade under the bent metal and very carefully worked the bit of rock free. For once the mule's contrary nature did not present a kick, but Blue still stepped back fast as he put the hoof down. This particular mule was more than handy with those hind legs. He clucked at the son and studied the two uncertain strides. Tha was enough.

An hour later the small band limped to the side per of a ranch calling itself the Line 40. Said so on the sigr up over the shed door. Blue felt like he should keep checking his back, as if he'd done something wrong and his hand stayed firm on the handle of the pistol. Be unfriendly to take out his ancient Henry, but he wished he had the comfort of its power in his hands.

The place looked deserted. Good. Blue's better sense was getting to him; he knew he never should have ridden in here. Just so damned hungry to hear a voice And for all its fancy naming, this ranch was a cousir to those he'd worked for so many years. Hardscrabble just getting by, and mean. Blue expected to see that dirty-faced old man come crabbing around the barn corner. It was time for him to leave. He put rein to the buckskin and started the turning circle.

Until a big man came around a corner, a man whose face and manner eased his nerves. A man well into six feet, with wrinkled lines around his mouth, and bright blue eyes. Older some, pushing fifty years, wearing a clean shirt and britches pegged into knee-high mule-eared boots. Looked something suspicious to Blue, but the words came out all fine and friendly. Blue sure enjoyed their sound.

"Well, how do there son. Good to see company this far out. You just step right down from that big feller and get yourself a cup 'a good coffee. Missus 'bout due to set dinner on the table. Be right glad to have you join us."

Blue liked those words, especially the part about the eating. Guess he was still a growing boy at heart, even if he was twenty-one. He looked around one more time, real quick-like, not wanting to insult his host. There was nothing wrong that he could see, but there was an unrest poking at his mind and worrying him.

The big man slapped the buckskin gelding, barely looked over the mare and colt, and joined in the misery about the mule's twisted shoe. "Can fix that right after we eat, son. No problem at all. Glad to be a help." The sounds rubbed over the worry in Blue's mind, easing his conscience enough to let him put up the horses.

There was hay and water for the mule and the stolid

buckskin in two piles at a hitching line, and an empty pen for the mare and foal. It was a high-walled pen shaded at one end, with a hayrick holding the sweetest hay Blue'd seen in a long time. Just waiting there for the mare and foal. He shook his head and followed the big man into the house.

Dinner was waiting there, spread out on a long table almost too pretty for speaking. More food than he'd seen in a long time. The women, they were pretty, too. A wife, so it seemed to Blue, and two girls younger than him. One of them had a wall-eyed look, and the other stared at her feet, but they were young and clean and smelled pretty to Blue.

The introductions never got to names for the women. "I be Noah Carlson, son, owner of this Line 40. Runs all the way down into the Territory. Good land, good graze. And you be . . . ?"

Blue made his manners as fast as he could, wanting to get to the eating. But the old man made to bow his head in prayer and talk on about their new friend and their multitude of blessings. The wall-eyed daughter had the advantage. Blue couldn't tell if she was looking at her folded hands or sideways at him.

The meal didn't last long enough. When it looked like there wouldn't be enough for all to eat, the women stopped, pushing their plates away in unison. Blue made a choking protest as the old man laughed and handed him another biscuit. Blue didn't have the heart to disappoint him.

The old man could talk. He rambled on about his

and, about the stock he planned to raise, the fast orses and wild times of days gone by. He finally got o asking the question just as Blue was getting into the ast piece of dried apple pie.

"That there mare you hauling along. She's something fancy, 'pears to me. Easy to see she got good lood in her, and the colt's a good one. What you loing with them. No offense meant, but you look too oung and down on your . . . hell, you know what I'm aying. To own quality stock like them two."

Blue knew better, but the heavy settling of the dinner neal and the luxury of fresh milk and sugar sweetening in his coffee shook loose his tongue and ummed up his judgment. It had been a long time—onsidering his past, a real long time—since he'd sat o dinner with nice folks and talked. And he was eginning to like the looks of the wall-eyed girl.

He spoke for a long time about the mare and his trip outh. Made it sound like something wild and dangerous. He kept glancing at the wall-eyed girl and ever really looked into the wide and friendly face of is host. Never saw the greed shine free in the twinkle f the blue eyes. He was enjoying the full feeling, the ethargy of a good meal, and the enchanting sound of is own voice.

The two men stepped out to the front porch, "to have smoke, don't want to bother the Missus none while he's clearing the table." The buckskin and the mule vere done with their dinner, but the mare was still vorking at her pile, a periodic lift and fall of the stumpy tail the only sign of life in the sleeping colt a her side. Blue leaned against the post supporting the sagging roof, worn out from the food and the talk. His elbow skidded off the rounded post, and he stepped forward to catch his balance.

Something shattered beside his head and he spun around, instantly knowing what was wrong, instantly back in the brightness of the world. The gun at his side came easily into his hand and settled waist-high and cocked. But the big man was fast and took another swing at Blue before he fired. Blue ducked down and drove himself forward into the exposed belly of his host. The axe handle thumped across his back but his charge put both men to the slatted floor. The big man rolled on him, ready to use his weight to keep Blue pinned. A knee to the crotch and two fingers jabbed into one eye loosened the grip, and Blue finished the roll, to end with him riding the full belly and cursing a wild streak.

He brought his right hand around in an arc, the pisto clenched in his fist. The big man tried to break his hold by bucking madly, lifting his butt and belly off the floor in desperate heaves, head rolling madly in frustration.

Blue was aiming for just above the left ear, but the big man's thrashing brought his head up and twisting to catch the gunsight squarely in the left eye. Blue heard the crack of bone, felt the scream start in the wide chest and tear through them both. The body went limp, the big hands let go their hold on Blue's throat and went to cradle the bloody face. Dark lines came from under the double-pressed hands, streaming into the man's wide open-mouth, running down his left arm and staining the snowy whiteness of his sleeve.

It was more than Blue had meant, more than the man deserved. Blue leaned to his left and grabbed at the post, pulled himself off the rocking body. He'd surely blinded that eye, tearing it and drawing out the fluid. There was a milky-white line mingling with the streaks of darkening blood.

Blue made it across the yard, patted the buckskin on the dark gold of his shoulder, and dropped to his knees to vomit. He was there a long time, holding to the quiet horse's leg, body frozen in a mockery of prayer. Voices from behind him told the story: high sounds of keening panic, low murmurs of comfort. The women left him alone in his private misery.

Some time later, perhaps thirty minutes, perhaps more, Blue pulled himself erect to bridle the gelding, tie the mule to the long black tail, and go to the mare. He would have to do something about the mule's hoof, to bend and reset the shoe. What he should have done earlier, instead of taking the crooked shoe as an excuse to seek out company. It would be a long time before he would welcome the sight of another human. Not until he reached the ranch way to the south of here.

★ Chapter 4

The scent carried on the wind and told him what to expect before the buckskin made the turn around the leaning rock and dropped to the unexpected lushnes of the small water hole. Blue felt tension come to the stolid horse as the gold neck came up, the black tipped ears pricked to touching. His own body stiffened in instinctive response to the warning smell.

Smoke. Harsh, acrid smoke with a tang foreign to his mountain senses. Everything down here was different. Hadn't started out that way up at Beaufort, but the las week saw the high grasses give way to growths o tough pointed bush, wide-spaced clumps of brittle brown grass, narrow spikes of sharp-branched trees The heat had come, too, roasting him under his winte hat, sticking the flannel shirts to his back and turning them black under his arms. Even the small canyons and flat plateaus were different.

But he knew the taste of smoke in the air meant men and they would be no different. Back ten miles or so he'd made a bad choice and was stuck with it. Stil spooked by his ride into the Line 40, Blue had tacked around a ranch and missed a well-traveled road which on the map, looked to head between two mountains And got himself trapped in country unmarked by the Señor. Three days he'd been working his way down the rough land, skipping over the crumbly, orange streaked rock, going wide around the spindly stalks o cactus. Twice he had to stop and pull a long spear from the colt's flank, but now it looked that the baby had learned to keep his distance.

Blue didn't like it. The smoke smell was straight ahead, and the only path he found to bring them out of the endless hills was high walled and narrow, penning them in till the bottom. He could see the beckoning green long before they had reached the small canyon, but the ride to it was a half-day's trip. And now, at the bottom, there was the smoke.

The pack mule was ten lengths behind him, placid and unmoved by the nearness of the greenery, the shimmer of water. But the mare was restless, pulling close to Blue's knee, shoving into the buckskin's shoulder. The colt's curiosity was getting to her. The chestnut was hidden under the massive gold neck of the patient buckskin.

Distracted by the smoke, Blue was too slow. He swung the buckskin hard left but missed the agile colt, who was under the neck and running down the remaining jumble of rock to the soft enticement of the grass. The mare jammed Blue's leg, shoved the buckskin hard off balance. Blue let the big horse go to his knees and rode lightly as the animal staggered up against the mare pulling sideways in panic.

He reached for the brown shiny neck and the mare shied at his hand, eyes white, ears swiveling rapidly to follow the colt. Blue cursed her under his breath and touched spur to buckskin, urging the horse against all common sense to come down the rest of the trail in one leap. The mare came in behind and Blue could no longer hear his own cursing above the clatter of the horses. The pack mule leaned back against the rope.

If there was any hope left the owners of the fire had not heard his arrival, the mare's high whinny drowned them. Now the whole territory knew his whereabouts. Blue kept the buckskin circling in a steady trot and reached back to unknot the mule's tail line. The chestnut colt thought it a great game and stayed just out of reach of his dam, just far enough to keep her at a high pitch.

Finally, Blue halted the buckskin, dragging the mare to a standstill. Worry turned the mare nasty and she snapped at Blue, tearing a long stripe of denim from his pants that left behind a multiplying line of beaded blood.

"God damn it, mare." The curse eased the tingle in his leg, but he never raised the soft sound of his voice. Rubbing his hand down the flesh, he smeared the droplets into the torn edge of the pants. Blue cursed again, holding this one under his breath. Then the chestnut colt found he was tired of the game and ready for late lunch. He found his dam and butted at her hind leg, impatient to get going.

"That old bitch got you good, didn't she, cowboy?" The voice spun Blue in the saddle, and he added a longer string of curses to his complaints. Then he settled the buckskin and took a good look.

It was only one man, and not much of one at that. But this time it was one man too many for Blue. The muscles along his neck and back eased some as he patted the buckskin and took the time to settle himself. If only this jasper showed, Blue figured he could handle things all right.

"Mighty nice looking lady you got there, cowboy. You headed somewheres in particular or just out riding for your health?"

Nosy son of a bitch. Blue swung his head side to side, searching for the other man. A quick sweep of the small canyon gave him nothing that was a threat. He focused on the man before him. The long time between his question and Blue's getting around to answer didn't seem to bother the gent. He sat on his spotted horse and smiled.

"Delivering her and the colt to their owner. Most there and surely am looking forward to getting out of this saddle, and this heat. Been a long ride."

That was more than he wanted to say but it had been a goodly time since his words had gone to something other than the horses and the disinterested pack mule. Better keep his mouth shut this time and wait the gent out. Blue was getting gun-shy of strangers.

The rider swung his right leg in front of him, hooking it to the high swell of the saddle, and then reached back into his saddle bag. Blue's hand went automatically to the butt of the Henry under his knee, and the man looked up slowly at the quickness of the movement. A smiled came across his pudgy face, revealing even, white store-bought teeth.

"No business for you to worry, cowboy. Just figured

iff'n you been riding a distance then you might be needing a smoke. Got extra fixings in my gear. Righ here."

Damn the man. Sounded good. A quick tug at the wrong moment from the mare had scattered his makings to the wind maybe eight days back. He'd missed the bitter taste that eased his worries, softened the loneliness. Even missed the simple act of rolling the paper and wetting it, then the extra twist. But another look into the wide, smiling face and Blue felt more alone. Nobody ever offered something for free.

This rider didn't seem to carry too much in height but he made up for it in the belly riding snug under his shirt and unbuttoned vest. A clean-shaven face showing the beginnings of stubble, gray hair slicked over a shiny balding head, and bright blue eyes almost hidden in creases folded against the sun. Whipcord trousers and fancy high-topped boots, a good store-bought shirt filthy from being worn too long. The clothes took away any menace in the man, but Blue plain didn't trust a man hanging around out here.

"You want that smoke, son? I got me enough here for you and a whole army. See any Indians while you was riding through? You crossed their big trail back there, you see any of them savages?"

The words slid over Blue, the unfamiliar sounds echoing in his ears. The urge for the smoke taste rose in him, battling with his knowledge that something was wrong. He touched his tongue to dry lips and imagined the feel of hot and bitter smoke. Smoke.

Something was seriously wrong. He shook his head, strange blue eyes flickering side to side. All his nerves told him to run. But where?

The buckskin head rose quickly, the mare took a step away from the sleeping colt, and Blue had that moment to see the pleasure cross the strange man's face. Then he felt the pull of a rope settle across his shoulders, draw his arms useless against his chest. He cursed his slow stupidity, his voice rising with the anger, and then he went sliding over the broad rump of his horse to hit the hard ground.

There was a moment when he could hear nothing but his lungs pumping in his ears, struggling to pull in enough air through cramped muscles. Then he began to sort out the sounds coming from the fat man standing over him. And they weren't good to hear.

"Cowboy, you ain't even dry behind the ears yet. Likely never will be. Can't figure why the almighty Señor Maldinado let the likes of you bring that bit of fancy horseflesh down here. You ain't got the good sense the Lord gave a jackrabbit."

The rising laughter rubbed at Blue, digging the insult in deeper, the more painful because it was true. He fought to come to his knees and reach the red face to wipe out the stinging sounds. He made it halfway, then a voice, somehow familiar, stopped him, left him bent double.

"Quit it, sonny. Ain't nothing you can do now." The rope eased some of its pressure. Blue straightened slowly and looked around. Off to one side he could see the buckskin, grazing comfortably on the sparse grass. The mare was alongside, matching the gelding bite for bite. The outline of the colt was just visible, flat out on the ground, sides rising and falling in sleep. That son could sleep through anything when the urge hit him.

The voice. Blue looked at the fat man, saw the smile, watched the eyes go beyond him. He knew the man behind him from somewhere. The rope loosened. Blue wondered if it was deliberate. Didn't matter, it was his only chance.

The release gave him room. Blue ducked his head into the loop and raised his arms to turn the rope free, then came up in a wild lurch to slam into the still-grinning fat man. The rush of breath gagged him as they rode to the ground. A quick succession of blows to the round face and Blue felt the body sag beneath him. Too easy.

He was right. In the long timeless seconds Blue saw the three animals raise their heads at the antics, saw the foal rise quickly at an unseen signal from his dam, saw the buckskin pull away uneasily from the schooling of his trailing reins.

Out of the side of his eye Blue felt the long arc of the barrel flash beside him before he knew the power of the blow. He was unconscious before he rolled to the ground.

There was no sense of time when he first heard the sounds. Words, curses of hot anger. Then hoofbeats going away, becoming faint, then more coming back

Words, stronger curses. Blue fought to lie still, to keep his eyes closed and listen.

"No good." The words came between deep breaths as if the speaker had worked hard. "Gone, all 'a them. Not a sight. Tracks went down into the wash, caught up in a herd come down to water. Then went back out to the hard rock. No goddamn sign."

"Damn." A boot toe caught Blue in the ribs, raising him and then dropping him. He bit into the side of his mouth and held back the groan that wanted out. Then the toe came again, harder this time, and digging into his neck. He forced himself limp, tightened his closed eyes, drew more blood from his shredded cheek. He could feel the thin trickle slide out of his mouth to spread through soft whiskers. The voices started again.

"One good thing. Them broncs don't know the territory. So they sure 'nough won't drift to the Single M. But I sure wanted that mare's head. Planned on hanging her upside the sign. Let that damned greaser know what we think on him."

The other voice, the familiar voice in this alien land, started in. "Well, to hell with that mare. This here's the son I wanted. Got him, too. Nice and pretty, lying there. What you want doing with him now, Vace? Ain't going to just ride off and leave the bastard here."

Blue gave himself the luxury of a small sigh. They wouldn't hear it over their own talking. Something to do with the horse, yet the one man had wanted him in particular. No one down here knew him, but the voice held in his mind. He almost let his eyes drift open.

There was a whisper of sound. Then the voice again "Best kill the son of a bitch and leave him here. Tha there daughter of his comes riding up here some days Let her find the corpse, let her take the word home to daddy."

Blue rolled frantically, but the impact of the bulle came before the explosion blossomed in his head There was no pain, only a growing numbness in his chest that drove away the fractured sounds and bright-ened inside his head to shut out the day. He tried once to move against the paralyzing numbness, and thought for a moment he had stood up to the bitter laughter of his killers. Then even that idea faded and he did not hear the two horses as they were ridden from the smal canyon, their riders slumped in the saddle, the fat man reaching behind him for the bottle.

Then even the light was gone, and a coldness settled in the small and remote high canyon.

★ Chapter 5

The words stayed clear in her mind. Even as she sad-dled the restless yellow mare, reaching for the latigo strap and doing up the cinch by feel. It was unrea-sonably cold in the predawn, and the soft light put a blurred edge to the shapes around her as she moved by instinct through the low-roofed shed. The old mare pretended to snap at her hands when she slipped the high port bit into the already open mouth, and the girl laughed at the nonsense. But the words of her father pushed aside the small moment of pleasure.

"There is trouble, little one. Men who are looking to put the Indian back behind bars, to capture him and move him from his lands. They are angry that we let him ride the land behind us, as if we could put up a fence and keep him out. These men are angry, and their power is growing. They will do anything. So stay out of the hills, stay within sight of the open land and the house."

She could not believe that any threat against her father, anything to do with the Indians, would be passed down to her and her safety. No man would stop her from riding into her high rocked hills. It had come to her to argue with her father, but the lines around his mouth, the flat light to his eyes, warned her away from such folly. Her mother had taught her well. But she would still ride up into her hills.

The yellow mare swung her head and snapped at her mistress's arm, brushing long teeth across the tough leather brush jacket. This morning it was cool, unusual for the first week of the spring month. Celita swore a gringo oath under her breath, and swung into the old saddle without reaching for the stirrups.

It took her little time to reach the sharp beginnings of the hills that led to the Rincon mountains and the great San Pedro river basin beyond. If she rode high and fast before the sun broke free, she could dismount at the small catch basin beneath the trickle of water and see the quick changes of color as the sun found her valley below. There were better and faster horses on the ranch, but the ancient yellow mare had taken her up this trail for all the years of her life, and Celita found comfort in the presence of the quarrelsome animal.

There was only the sound of the small sharp hooves scrambling over the broken rock, the quiet sometimes broken by newly-angry birds scolding her for her intrusion. Celita reined in the mare. There was the still cry of a coyote, an answer across the valley. She forced the mare to step quicker, to beat the sun to the base of the steep trail.

The yellow mare made the last twist that brought them down into the canyon to the coldness of the waterfall. Celita's small body leaned forward in the mare's descent, her eyes scanned the ground. She was surprised; there was much sign of activity, hoof prints, some fresh, and even those of a mule. And shod horses. Few bothered to come up this high, with or without their riders.

Her slight weight was jolted sideways in the saddle as the yellow mare stopped unexpectedly, hindquarters still on the upswing of the track. The yellow head came up and the mare nickered softly. A dark horse turned its head in answer; a foal peeked out from the offside in curiosity. A dark buckskin head came up to stare at the intruder, high pommeled saddle still in place on the broad back.

Someone had lost two good horses and a wonderful foal. Celita's schooled eye quickly appraised the animals, delighting in the clean lines to the mare, the quickness to the colt. The dark mare came forward with eager steps to block the chestnut colt from racing to greet the newcomers. The buckskin only shook his head and went back to stripping the thin grass.

Celita gasped, then cried out. The sound stopped the curious foal who was turned back by a series of bites from his mother. Beyond the two grazing horses lay a body. A man, on his back, arms thrown wide, legs spread, face pale. Blood soaked through the sun-faded shirt and covered his chest and belly, staining to the waist of his torn denim pants, coming in lines from his ribs to drain into the pebbled ground.

Celita spurred the yellow mare in a series of bucks that brought her to the motionless form. Quick to kneel by the man, she saw a black rimmed hole high in his left chest, blood dried in a crusted mound that did not quite stop the dark trickle coming from the wound. She touched a hand to his face and drew back in shock at the coldness of his skin.

She spoke harshly to herself, angered at her childish ways, then put her hand back to his face, to feel along his jaw to his neck, searching for the thin beat that would mean life. She found nothing but the coldness. Then she picked up an arm, fingers pressed tightly to the veins at the wrist, searching again. And still there was nothing. The arm dropped to the ground dully, raising a small puff. No signs of life, yet that small line of blood coming through the blackened crust was fresh, telling her that this one must be alive. He must be.

She sat back on her heels and studied the motionles body. A livid bruise covered the right side of his hea and disappeared into the thick blond hair. He looke young, the faded yellow tan of his hands and the re peeling on his face and nose telling her he had win tered away from the sun. The tanned and peeled tex ture of his skin contrasted with the stark whiteness o his forehead, and made him somehow more vulner able. He could not be dead.

A black shadow crossed the hard ground betwee her and the body. She saw that the sun had entered he valley without her notice, and she looked up into th brightness. Vultures, first only a pair, then three more then four, joined in the circling wait.

She could not leave him here. If she rode to the ranc alone, he would be pulled apart before they coul return. She looked over at the buckskin. The mar would never carry double: this horse would have to do The saddle blanket was gone, as was the bridle, but th saddle and the high roll tied behind it were intact Surely he would have a rope somewhere, a belt, some thing she could use to lead the buckskin. There was n rope coiled to the saddle. She could see that from here She cursed another gringo oath, louder this time, lou enough to send a landing vulture up in flight.

Celita went to the grazing horses with hope. Th mare shied away and whickered to the colt to follow The buckskin cautiously watched her approach, neve raising his head from the scant breakfast.

Talking softly, crooning a tuneless song, Celita

earched the thin bedroll and saddlebags. No belt, no xtra bridle, but a pair of mended woven reins that vould be enough to wrap around the golden neck. The uckskin paid her no attention as she tied the old eather around him, but refused to step forward with er when she gave a gentle tug on the line. She cursed he stubborn horse and punched him in the belly. He ighed and followed her to stand over the body.

The girl was just sixteen and of slender build, but he had worked and ridden all her life. It took her ten ninutes of rolling the limp form, struggling with her ands locked across his bloody chest, but she finally ased the body onto a waist-high rock. Then she led he curious horse closer to the rock, positioning him arefully to stand broadside. A hand wiped across her ace brought the sight of the blood covering her arms oo close. She wanted to scream at the warm slickness ut she was silent, afraid that noise would spook the lready restless buckskin.

The horse felt her fears and sidestepped once, dropping the body hard on the slanted rock. Celita braced t against her knees and pushed and rolled the limp ody back to a leaning position, then halfway onto the addle, feet first. She refused to think any more that he burden was a human being; it had become a roblem of strength and determination.

Her calm voice steadied the buckskin, and she ooked one of the boots around the horn, then kept the orse in place with gentle hands and crooning words. She slipped under the heavy neck, hugging the horse's smell to her and taking its strength. On the other side she could grab the protruding foot, balance the leg on the slick leather of the worn saddle, and pull.

She pulled hard and the body did not move. The buckskin shifted against her tug. The body slipped down the rock. She pulled again, then released and pulled once more. A tearing noise came as the shoulders slipped from the rough surface. She leaned into the free hanging weight, digging her heels in for leverage.

The length of legs finally came over the saddle, one boot toe catching her on the chin. The buckskin moved again, this time away from her pulling, sliding the body further onto the saddle. Celita felt it herself as the loose-hanging head slapped against the fender of the near side of the saddle. It was as if she herself had been slapped. But the body was settled on the patient buckskin's back. Then the horse took one step, and the body threatened to slide back to the ground.

A shirt. Torn into strips she could tie 'it' securely in the saddle and lead the horse down the steep trail. There were shirts in the saddlebags. She remembered them from her search. They would have to do.

To dig back into the scanty gear that had once belonged to this lump of meat brought the man's life back to her. She looked into his face one more time. Fresh blood, coming from under the lifeless corpse trickled down the saddle skirting. He had to be alive.

Celita put her ear down to the face, gently turning the blood-smeared head so she could listen at his nouth. Very quiet now, almost afraid to hear some-hing, she knelt at the side of the horse and prayed as he waited.

A short sigh, a faint rattle deep in the throat. She vanted so badly to hear these things. Celita looked losely at the face, upside down to her, eyelids half-drawn back in the gently swinging head. He could not e alive still.

She saw a lid flutter. The thin dripping of blood split nd ran onto the golden coat. The gelding turned his ead and nipped at the tickling irritation, shifting the ody in the saddle, loosening Celita's hold on the rms. She had to move quickly. The shirt came apart in er hands in wide strips, and she tied the hands and eet to the big cinch rings. A few more strips were notted from the belt loops on his pants to the saddle orn. It was the best she could do and it would hold to he ranch. That was enough.

Before Celita mounted the yellow mare, she knelt ne more time to put her ear up against the parted lips, oping to hear what she thought had come to her efore. There was nothing this time. She brought the nd of one finger up to draw back an eyelid, and saw he deep blue-greenness of the eyes, blank and empty f sight. There was nothing in this man now, no signs, o stirrings. It must have been her imagination.

The yellow mare wanted to run. Her breakfast of weet hay and cool water waited at the ranch below. elita kept a tight hand on the reins and the obstinate ld mare settled into a shuffling, quick-stepping walk, head tossing with impatience at the measured slowness of the gait. The buckskin followed on a short lead. The dark mare and her curious foal came along with them, trotting in frantic spurts to get ahead, then resting and grabbing at mouthfuls of grass and milk.

There was no need to hurry. The burden draped over the back of the stolid buckskin was surely dead. Yet something pushed at the girl; something made her quicken the mare's steps the last half mile on the level ground. The brown mare responded as if to a challenge and galloped past with tail streaming over her back, head high, strides reaching for speed. The chestnut colt followed in great bucking leaps.

The shrill whinny of the mare as her offspring found horses in the mesquite pen brought men out of the long, low building. She stood in the center of the high-walled yard, eyes wild, turning and prancing in her effort to keep her foal in sight.

It was this scream that brought Rafael Maldinado away from his wife to stand on the flat dirt floor of the ramada and see the display of his prized mare. The colt frightened himself with the commotion he caused, and sought safety in the flanks of his mother. And there they stood for the Señor. No halter, no lead ropes, no pack mule, and no buckskin horse and long-haired rider. Rafael felt a sadness, a sense of loss that the wild-eyed cowboy had let him down.

It was his daughter's voice that took his gaze away from the beauty of the mare and the chestnut colt. Julio valked towards the mare with a loop of rope in one and.

"Papa, come quick. I have found someone. I think he s dead, I hope . . .

The words stopped, swallowed with tears, as her ather reached the yellow mare and took hold of the ridle. Celita slid from the still-walking mare and went ack to grab the buckskin. Rafael let the yellow mare o, and she went straight for her single pen and vaiting breakfast.

Rafael went with his child. He needed to look only nce at the swinging head to know. There was a band ightening across his chest. He looked up and across he blood-stained back to his daughter's face. Her vords refused the evidence of his eyes and his years.

"He may be alive, Papa. He may be. There was a reath, and there is still fresh blood. Look. Please. Get ome men, get some help. Where is Mama? We must ake him to the house and care for his wound. Please, apa?"

She must know. Rafael nodded to his child and verted his eyes, unwilling to see the hope in her face. Yes, they would carry this one to the house and put im down gently; yes, they would care for his wounds. But there would be no medicines, no ointments and andages, only the traditional washing of the corpse, he fresh clothes, the candles around his head. And urial tomorrow in a high narrow grave.

Three men stepped from the crowd to work loose the ashing of the body. The dark leather of the saddle was shiny in the bright sunlight, slick from blood soake into its seat and skirting. Perhaps Celita was righ There must be some life or there would no longer b fresh blood.

Rafael looked down at the gray face, the lips a thi blue line, the eyes rolled back in their sockets showing only the clear white under half-opened lids He touched fingers to the left side of the neck, to th spot under the jaw, then to the upturned wrists, crosse with faded dark lines and pale white in the day. Ther was nothing he could find.

He did not look at his daughter then, but shook hi head against her hopes. The men carried the body t the house, to the small back room off from the kitcher the room that had held others such as this. They lai the body down very gently and left the darkened roor quickly.

A woman appeared in the doorway to the smal room. Basin and cloth in hand, she walked slowl across the hard, tiled floor to stand over the body Slight in build, auburn hair pinned up and covered b a dark kerchief, she waited beside the young girl. I was only when she stood next to her grown daughte that the age of Ruth Perry Maldinado becam apparent: the thickening at the waist, the tracing o lines at her eyes and mouth, the barest sag to he throat. And it was standing next to each other that th connection between them was evident: the tilt to thei heads, the clarity of the hazel eyes, the smudges o freckles.

Ruth sent her husband from the room and leaned ently into her daughter's side, taking the trembling ıto her own body. She smiled at her child, then took moment to wipe with the dampened cloth at the treak of tears on the dusty face.

"Celita, you will help me now. It is time you learned. 'his is the other side of living. Child, come here with ıe, help me to remove the shirt. You will have much ıme for the tears later."

Despite her words, she found the tears pressed hard gainst her own eyes. He looked so young, this one, too 'oung for the killing mark of the blackened hole high ı his chest. But she had seen younger men than this rought home with such holes. And much worse. She topped for a short moment to wipe at her own tears.

And to watch her daughter. Watch her Celita dip a loth in the cooling water in the basin and wipe at the usted stains on the exposed flesh. Their eyes met cross the whiteness of the flesh. The pity showed on heir faces. So thin, with ribs too easy to find under earching fingers, the muscles slack and too close to he bone. The hard use this one had seen, too much for ne who had lived such a short life. A muffled cry ame from Celita. Her mother only shook her head in varning and dipped a cloth again in the pink water.

'here had been no pain. Not yet. He had to concentrate n breathing, to spend what strength he had to force hallow gasps from his frozen lungs. Just enough air to eep himself alive.

He had been taken somewhere. He had smelled the familiar warmth of the horseflesh near his face, had felt the tugging and the pulling, but as if it were done to someone else. Only once had he been able to make a sound, to force air between his clenched teeth and shape words. It was against the tearing in his chest, the pain high inside him.

The noise had echoed hard in his ears, like thunder. But there had been no answer, as if he had not spoken. Then he retreated back inside his mind, barely conscious of the hands holding him, touching him. He knew the sway of the horse, the rapid unknown talking, and more of the touching. Then the cool wetness on his flesh.

The touch of the cold brought him back to trying. A stiff breath forced itself through his jaw, a surprising stab of pain answered deep in his chest. His body suddenly demanded more air, and he drew even deeper breaths as the pain inside him grew and he struggled to resist its growth. Finally a cry came from him, a cry of rage against the building fire.

And finally he heard words above him, understood what they were saying.

“Mama, he is alive. I know it. Papa.” The sound trailed off into a piercing cry.

★ Chapter 6

He knew the trip to town was a necessity. He could no onger find acceptable excuses for the empty flour arrel or the lack of sugar and shortening. The hard ush of work was done, the cattle turned out on ummer range up in the high plateau between the nountains. The mares were bred and settled, the yearing colts cut, the two- and three-year-olds started. There was nothing left that allowed him to remain way from the town.

A surge of anger rose in him. It was his valley, his ome for the forty-five years of his life. And now there vere anglos who said that they owned the adobe-valled village of Tucson, and that he, Rafael Maldnado, was no longer welcome there. Perhaps even the ick gringo in his own house would deny him access o what he had fought to build. The foolishness of such bsurd anger brought a barking laugh from him. The oy was still sick, too sick to do more than sip warm roth and roll his eyes when someone spoke to him. And yet he, Rafael Maldinado, was putting into the nnocent youth the bitter actions of his countrymen.

There were still some who welcomed him, and many who would trade with him. Stevens, Warner, even Brown and Ronquist. The railroad brought in more oods each trip, more trading stock that was stiffer ompetition at lower prices. So the Maldinado money vas good, even if the name was not. He grinned at the

irony of frontier justice. The railroad these powerfu
men had fought to bring their town was now killin
them with its cheap transportation of goods.

Then he sobered quickly. It was not only his nam
and his heritage, it was his life that the gringos dis
trusted. Living here at the base of the mountains, sur
viving untouched by the indios that had terrorized th
vast plains of the Sonora desert for the past twent
years, and married to one of their own, a youn
woman with auburn hair and hazel eyes. This stuck i
their throats and kept the words rolling against Rafae
Maldinado. But these men could not hurt him wit
their words.

Still, he was reluctant to ride into their town. H
could not deny that to himself. He saddled an
mounted the brown gelding. The list that Ruth ha
given him was folded twice and tucked into his ves
pocket. It had been several trips since she had com
with him into Tucson. The first soft insults turne
quickly into ugly words, and she chose to stay at hom
and keep a rifle nearby. She had good men with he
Annuncio, who had helped to deliver Celita; an
Mickey, who knew the ways of the indios and coul
fight the best of them. She was safer in the hills tha
she was in the civilization of Tucson.

The anger crowded his good sense, and he drov
spurs into the sleek sides of the brown gelding. Th
anger rode with him as the horse ran from the hard
packed yard, pulling the two pack animals into a lum
bering run. Their sheer weight slowed the eage

elding, and brought some sanity back to Rafael's ioughts.

The fourteen miles to town would take him almost ntil evening. Then he would give his list to Warner t the Mercantile and spend the evening visiting with iose few who did not turn away from him. omorrow he would be home by midafternoon. As sual, he chose not to ride with a wagon and team long the easier route, the beginnings of a road carved ut through the mountains by the miners in the San edro valley wanting their supplies from Tucson. He id not like the slow encumbrance of the draught am and heavy farm wagon. He had a need for the eady surge of the horse beneath him to soothe the onstant anger.

Rafael looked back once to the low, slanted lines of ie hacienda, the ramada shielding the deep-set win-ows from the summer sun. The tightly woven iesquite fencing held only a few horses now; his ders were up in the high valley with the stock. Then e turned to the land ahead of him. A few more miles t a steady trot, and he could see the high rise of dust om the road angling in beside him. There would be ie creek crossing, and then the path he rode would onverge with many others to form their own road to ucson. Two years past he would be making this trips ith an armed escort, for both Indians and bandits ode the wide valley. Now he was safe enough alone. or a while. There were a few benefits from the rapid oread of the city and its claim to civilization.

• • •

But the claims were not enough to offset the fur rising in him as he walked the brown gelding throug the streets of Tucson. Stores had come up in grea numbers, offering wide selections to the curious traveler. Books, meats, ladies apparel, goods beyond th necessities. Most of those on the street barely glance at him, looking only long enough to recognize his heritage. Those whom he recognized, who had once bee his friends, frowned and turned their heads, the gestur acknowledging their betrayal.

Warner's store, and the two other shops on the stree he rode through, were housed in the thick, ancier adobe that had been a part of the town from its beginnings. Rafael laughed. Now the gringos were trying t impose their former lives on the desert city, the live they had left willingly to come to this distant outpos He had ridden past two of the new houses. They di not belong: houses with thin wooden walls, wide glas windows rising high above the ground, letting in th killing sun. Houses set back from the street, trying t sit graciously on wide expanses of lawn, trying to tam the dust with green grass. He could only shake hi head at the folly. This change in the style of livin would cost a great deal, both to the builders an owners of these great houses, and to the land they wer trying to tame.

The afternoon was late, and there were no horses a the railing before Warner's store. Rafael ducked unde the long tie rail and took the few steps that brougl im to the heavy glassed door. He could see only one ustomer inside, an unfamiliar face in a heavyset body. 'here was no one of importance here to challenge him.

He shook his head against the defeating thoughts. 'here was no reason he could not walk into any store ı this town and buy what he wished, without interfernce. But he had grown tired, and he did not like to ıink of Ruth and Celita alone at the sprawling ranch. Ie would hurry and return there.

Warner barely looked up as Rafael entered, and there ,as no greeting on the once open and smiling face. 'he lone customer paid him no mind, poking with disıterest through a pile of dark work pants. It was easy › hand the tall storekeeper his list and turn to go ,ithout exchanging words. He expected nothing from ıe sour man, and did not plan to wait for an insult. He ,as not prepared for the eagerness of his words.

"I heard you got a sick one at the ranch. Some rider ou hired up north, brought down that blooded mare. Vhat happened, you ever find out from him? How's e doing now? Talk is he still ain't going to make it. Iust be hard on the missus."

Such a long speech for the man, with almost friendly ,ords and a curious interest in their guest. Rafael ›oked to see if the other man had a share in the harmess gossip. But he was gone. So he allowed himself a mall shared grin with Warner, to acknowledge and ring back the friendship of the past.

"Yes, he is still with us. Almost four months now, and e is only half awake for most of the time. My Ruth does not mind as Celita is able to help her now. But sh had missed her visits with her friends in town, wit your Rosa. Perhaps when this trouble is settled . . .

But they both knew there would be no return. An there was a double irony in the situation. For th respectable Mrs. Warner was of Spanish descent, a were most of the wives of the early settlers. And thes ladies lived their lives completely in their husbands heritage, aloof from the working Mexicans.

The brief flare of kindness faded from Warner' eyes, and an edge of coldness came back to the man At the same time, Rafael became aware of anothe presence in the darkening room. Warner reached ove his head and twisted a knob on the light fixture, t bring the gaslight up to brighten the hollow room. On more of the benefits of the growing city.

"What you talking about there, Señor? We hear about your man. No need for a white man to be stayin with you. No need at all. Don't want to bother th missus. We'll be up with tomorrow's light to pick hin up. Sure enough, there ain't no need at all."

Rafael turned slowly, knowing beforehand what fac would greet him. A wide round face with gray hai carefully combed over the shining skull, a bell pushing at the one button holding the fancy leathe vest. Vace Yarborough. A man who rarely worked an had more than enough.

And there was a new one standing with Vace, th heavy shape and dirty clothing telling Rafael ho Yarborough had found him so easily. He nodded to th hickset man and was rewarded with a flush to the vhiskered face. There was some feeling to the dull-yed man.

Vace wasn't going to be upstaged by his own man. "You listening, we'll take that man you got up there. in't enough to let them Indians ride your land, don't eed to be put out by some no-count kid. Ain't right."

There was never a direct threat to Vace's words, ever an outright insult, but the man knew the combi-ations that drove the words deep into Rafael without ulling blood. It would do no good to tell Vace one nore time that he never had control over the Indians, hat no one man could stop them from using the arrow trail along the San Pedro river and through the igh graze. It would always be Geronimo's to use, to ide in and out of the desert toward Mexico. Yarbor-ough and his cronies would never comprehend the vords.

Rafael turned his back to the two men. "Warner, I vill be back to pick up my stores midmorning. Vace, ou are a fool with your words that mean nothing. Let ne pass."

Yarborough's hands went up in a placating gesture f abject surrender. He knew the limits, knew how far e could push and not get called out.

"Well, now, Señor. No call for anger here. Just trying o be of service. No need at all."

Vace had no interest in facing the proud man whose and rested knowingly on the butt of a smooth-han-lled revolver. Everyone knew of Maldinado's reputa-

tion, and his temper. This unborn fight would grow i
Vace's direction later, on his terms, on his ground.

So Yarborough elbowed Bristol Adderson hard in th
meaty ribs, getting a surprised grunt from the slow
witted man. Then Vace stepped back with a flourish
making a wide sweep with his hand and arm. Le
Warner sell to the dirty greaser for now. But that, too
would end soon enough.

There were two men in Tucson who would welcom
Rafael into their homes. Two men who had come t
the growing city when it was a walled village, sur
rounded by unbroken lands and clean mountains. Nov
they were no longer men of importance, losing thei
power and their fortunes to the gamble of the railroa
and the younger, stronger men. But to Rafael and hi
wife, they remained constant friends.

It took Henry Wallem and Bates Weston most of th
evening to convince Rafael not to return to Warner's a
his leisure in the morning for his goods, but to get ou
and be gone before the fullness of the dawn. Waller
found the clinching argument, one he knew his frien
would understand.

"You heard this nonsense about the 'Meson Ring,
about some men stirring up the Indians and the
calling for help from the government and the soldiers
Well, it ain't just a wild story for the papers to peddle
Someone is making big money selling extra goods
feeding the special troops, outfitting the scouts an
patrols. They want this Indian trouble kept going, lon

s it don't come close to them. They got a case against ou, stirring up the town's folks, 'cause it's known ieronimo rides up in back of you. They want your anch, damnit, and they want someone up there yelling or help loud and clear. You take care now, stay here ne night and be on your way come early morning, efore that Yarborough gets moving. That'll get you ome in one piece this time."

Rafael listened to his friends, heard their words of varning, and thought of his moments with the smiling 'arborough. He waited out the night, restless and lone in the high feather bed. It was still dark, the high nountains to the east blocking out the new morning un, when he rose.

The 'Tucson Ring' be damned. Rafael would never neak around this town again. He would complete his elf-imposed rout this time, he would pack the goods Varner promised to leave inside the safety of the back f his store, and he would run from the town this time. But never again.

The two pack horses objected to the early hour, to ne high stacking of the goods, but Rafael kneed the ne too-quarrelsome gelding in the gut and pulled the ope tighter across the canvas. This time they might ave to run part of the way. Running home. It went gainst his pride, his whole being, to run. Just this one ime, until he could know the safety of his wife and his hild. Then the town and its bought and paid for anger vould remember the strength of Rafael Maldinado.

The brown was as eager as his rider to make the

journey home. The horse pulled the mutinous pac horses at an unwilling jog to the banks of the muddie creek. Instinct made Rafael pull up before committin himself and his load to the shallow ford. It was early too early for most in this town to have already crosse into the valley on legitimate business.

He stared at the dense thicket of mesquite an cactus, bright green palo verde and darker gree grasses. Trails split and ran through the wide valle from here. And it was well known that Rafael Mald inado would travel this rugged trail rather than th more level dust of the miners' road.

But not this time. He kneed the brown to the left an put the eager horse to a lope. He could feel the sof rope tighten across his thigh, could hear the nois bounce of the loaded pack horses as they struggled t find their footing. Once on the narrow bridge, Rafae stopped and looked down along the windin streambed. Back where he made his usual crossin there were two men putting their horses into the wate They had entered from the east, away from the city. I was two men whose faces he could not see, but whos heavy bulks sat deep in their high saddles.

One of them would be Vace Yarborough. And b now the man would be cursing, filling the air with hi unused anger. His companion could well be the sulle man from Warner's store. Rafael was tempted to lift hand in salute to the men, but instead he reined th brown toward home.

He did allow a smile. The sun was reaching to th

ops of the mountains ahead of him. It would touch the ile roof of the adobe ranch first. With the early start, ie would be home in time for dinner.

★ Chapter 7

His face red with unexpelled fury, Vace Yarborough anked the slow-moving paint around, slamming the vide-rumped horse into Adderson's blocky dun. His yes weren't that bad, and in the clear light of the early norning, he'd seen that hand rise as if to mock him in alute. Vace had to admit that this time the Señor had utfoxed him. It would not happen again.

Damn. His temper finally exploded and he started on cussing streak that got through Adderson's whiskey-ogged brain.

"You think the greaser saw us, Vace? You think he igured what we was after?"

Adderson was good with figuring out the obvious. The sheer brilliance of the questions settled Vace's emper for the moment, and he grinned wickedly at his iew partner.

"Yeah, Bristol, the Señor knows something was vaiting for him in that scrub, and he was just smart nough to hit the bridge and head for home. We drove im out too early this time, but that ain't no never-nind. We'll get him another time. There ain't no hance to that."

Adderson still didn't understand what the fancy mex ad to do with getting his hands on that runny-nosed kid. In fact, the mex had treated him pretty good on th trip down. At least the trail boss had; old Hack Light foot had been hard with the work and generous wit the grub. The three-week drive paid him well, an Bristol had enough ready cash after payday that he' had one high and wide time in the back streets o Tucson. Not a bad town, and friendly people, espe cially them dark-skinned females in Gay Alley. A fe pesos bought him a lot of woman down here.

Bristol dug his fingers into one armpit; goddamn th itching he got now. By God, he'd been flat down whe he shoved his way up to the long and crowded bar an tried to wheedle just one little drink from th whiskered bartender behind the long, splintere wooden barrier. Just one little drink.

The barkeep turned him down. Flat. Never min that he, Bristol Adderson, had spent most of his driv cash drinking through the two days at this here pa ticular bar. Nope, no give to that man, not even shake of the head. He'd just looked for the hard coi in Bristol's hand and turned away when he kne there would be none. The memory twisted at Bristol' narrow mouth.

Now his neighbor at this here bar, why, he turned ou to be right friendly. 'Merican, plain enough, and gen erous with the offer of a drink. Then the offer of shared bottle. Bristol liked the man's style. A goo man, Vace Yarborough, even with his mean tempe and fancy words. A man that listened to a long story. man to ride with. Bristol eased himself into the saddl

Ie was set now. Vace would tell him what to do next. Ie waited for the words.

What was going through Bristol's lame mind was ·asy reading for Vace. The man was a big dog, eager o do any master's bidding. What luck, to find the man lrunk and broke in that dirty bar. The bum had talked asily, almost too easily, going on about his fight with hat dumb cowpoke up in Beaufort, the long drive lown. And the fact that the kid was coming down by imself, leading the mare and her fancy offspring. 3ristol was hurting to get his own back from the kid. Jave Vace a damned good idea.

He was looking for his edge, for his entry into the mall circle of the Ring. Some folks said they was nade up, that there weren't no 'Ring' to control the olitics and stir up the Indians. But Vace knew better. Ie figured if he took the Señor out then entrance to the Ring and its wealth would be open to him.

Almost had him this morning, and lost him. The bit-erness wiped out the pleasure of his musings for Vace. Iis features turned in with hatred and he slapped his alm hard against the paint's neck, spooking his own orse and setting Bristol's roman-nosed dun to umping sideways, almost dumping the big lard of lesh. Bristol's rough scrambling to keep the saddle rought a harsh laugh from Vace. This was the best he ould do for a partner, the only backup man he had. Vhat made the man valuable was his set hatred for the id lying up at the greaser's—the kid they'd almost ot up in the hills—and the knowing that Bristol would side with him whatever. An easy man to throw away after the deed was done. Didn't want the Ring thinking they had to put up with Adderson's thick headed antics. Vace was looking forward to the day.

It took Blue a long time of staring up at the dark shapes before he could figure them out. Never seen anything like them before. Long spindly things that looked too weak to be holding up the ceiling above him. Since he was lying down and the long shapes went across the room from wall to wall, crosshatched by wooden beams, he figured it to be the ceiling.

The beams he recognized from the succession of rough built cabins in the high mountain country that he had suffered as home. But he'd never seen anything quite like this ceiling before. There was going to be a lot of new things he'd never seen before.

It was something to ask the pretty girl when she came back. He remembered one time to try and form the question, but nothing came out. No sound, no words. She had stared down at him, watching his face contort with the effort, then put a hand gently to his forehead, holding him back down on the soft pillow.

Damned silly letting such a skinny female hold him down with only one hand. But his attempt at protest brought a bitter pain to his chest and the return of the darkness.

It took him three more tries and God knows how many days before he got enough air in him to ask the question again. And he still didn't understand the answer. Spoke something different down here, thought he thought the girl was talking American. Guess it was Mex like he never heard before. Anyway, she finally said it was ribs from some big monster. Still didn't know if it was animal or tree. Or a man they plumb didn't like. Strange country he was in.

In time, Blue began to remember. Those last few days, when the buckskin hit the split in the high ground and lengthened his stride. They'd passed near to one town marked on the map, the town Blue chose to ride around and got lost doing. Crossed the new mining road too. No sign of anyone there. But once the buckskin got into the high pricklies, Blue let him pick his way, long as they was headed west. Been going south too long.

He'd never seen anything like it. The wide river valley lay behind them when they got into a high flat grassland that the horses didn't ever want to leave. Then through a tangle of rock and hard scrambles that brought them to the down side of the mountains. Below, way out below and across the flat valley, Blue had seen a light green that could be graze, but up here was nothing but all kinds of prickly bushes, and too many of them. Ground spreading pricklies that reached out to jump at a horse's belly; soft pale green pricklies that burrowed into the tail. Got the mule to bucking one time, quite a noisy sight. The worst was the barrel-shaped ones, squatty growing things with barbed hooks that really took hold. Had a hell of a time when the mare got into one of those. She liked to tear his arm off with the pain.

There were others almost beyond the height of a man, and higher. Holding out arms at a rigid salute. Barbed too, like the rest of them. Standing on a small bottom, swelling up and out to their great height. Some were half dead, flesh rotted away, ribs exposed just like a man's.

Ribs. Godalmighty. Blue attempted to sit up, taken by his discovery. Those long round shapes hanging over his head were the ribs from the big pricklies. He grinned through the tickle of pain; made good sense to build with what you had handy. And it had been a long sight between any stand of big trees. Had to climb higher into the mountaintops for a sight of timber.

Standing might not be so tough now. Blue swung his legs out from the light covering and planted both feet on the cool flooring. That, too, was different. Not bare dirt, not rough planking, but hard glassy squares. He looked down past his pale shanks to see the startling contrast of long feet and yellowed toenails on the deep shiny red of the floor. Different, yeah, and pretty. Beat swept dirt all to hell.

Standing was the next step. A quick grin came and went at his own expense. Couldn't be dying, not with that bad a joke. He ran a hand across his face and knew for certain that he'd been well cared for. No beard, not even short fuzz, and no nicks or scrapes. Whoever was doing the barbering was good. He shook his head gently and found the length of his mane shortened considerably. No swing to it. Someone was trying to civilize him while he slept.

Probably figured it to be the only way it would get done.

His searching fingers rasped across the roughened texture as he stood up into the support of the closest wall. He inspected this wall at eye level, finding it hard to get enough air to stand alone, then realized his chest was heaving, panic building in him. Something loud and angry came into his shrinking world.

A voice, a sound of long skirts, something familiar in his strange world of brown-ribbed ceilings and glass floors.

"Señor, you are not to be up. There is still much infection in you. Please to lie back down and rest."

A hand on his shoulder pushed down firmly, guided him to the easy comfort of the high bed. Blue thought to argue and almost got the words past his open mouth, but a slender finger crossed his lips.

"I do not want to hear those words. You have argued enough. Lie still."

This time it wasn't hard to give in and do what he was told. Small hands quickly pulled the light sheeting up around his shoulders and then sought out his face, touching his forehead firmly, resting there for only a moment, then whisking lightly across his mouth. He looked up into the almost familiar face, and was shocked.

He remembered bits of her from his waking moments. At least he thought it was her. Black hair colored like a bird's wing, shiny enough to have its own light. Strong angular face softened by the improbability of freckles, scattered across her nose and high on her cheeks, freckles that belonged to fair skin and chestnut hair. The eyes were a soft hazel green, like the high pines of his own mountains, not the soft brown or glossy black that lived with her dark hair. Must be confused with someone else, must be another woman here. Not just her.

She seemed to know his confusion. "You are safe here, Señor Blue. This is your home. I am Celita. I found you up at the canyon of the wild horses. And you are safe here."

He liked the name, liked the sound of the words that said he was safe. Something new for him. She touched her fingers one more time to his face, then Blue thought she smiled. But his eyes were closing against his will, and his last thought was of her smiling face.

There were other times when he woke up, other times he tried to stand. But each time hands and his own weakness pushed him back, while voices gave him orders. He gave up counting, almost gave up trying, but he kept the freckled face with the shiny black hair alive in his imagination. One of these times he would make it to his feet and find her. Find out if she was real.

Finally there were days he was left alone to walk around in his small room. The first time, one trip was all it took to send him back to the safety of the high bed. Then each day he could take more time on his feet, walk more times around the closeness of the room, counting the steps it took to complete the circle. One time around, then three times, then almost fifty times.

No one was there to stop him when he finally made it out of the small room back from the kitchen. Clean clothes, a loose white shirt, and soft faded pants had been hanging over the back of the chair for two days, waiting for his try. They were much too big on him but they covered him and that was enough.

There was only an old woman in the kitchen, and she wordlessly handed him a cup of the bitterest coffee he'd ever tasted. And that was saying something. She smiled at his rasping thank you and went back to her chores.

He guessed it would be midmorning. There was no one around outside. Standing under the long shed-row roof outside the door, he could look out over the wide land below. Same view as he'd had on his climb down to the small canyon. A whole state it seemed to him. Flat forever, broken only by the blue edge of ragged mountains clustered in small groups. But the flat land went around the peaks and out into the sun.

It came to him he didn't even know the time of year, and didn't know enough to make a guess. Didn't know how long he'd been here, what day or week or month. Hell, could even be the year, for all he knew. Been spring when he hired out to Señor Maldinado, took about a month for his trip down. Beyond that he didn't know.

It was too much. His mind spun, put him off balance

enough to drop the tin cup and reach for support. There was nothing here to recognize, nothing to tell him what was what. God, he'd been shot. That much he could remember.

His breathing came in short gasps, a familiar pain rose in his chest. Two steps back brought him against the coolness of the wall, a solid wall of simple mud. 'Dobe they called it. Now he remembered. The hard man with the gray streaked beard, the fawn-colored pants, and knowing eyes. The cell and then his freedom. The ride south with the special mare.

A wicked smile on a greasy face. And the shot that canceled everything. Shame rose in him. To be so stupid, to be caught out so easily by the grinning man and his unseen companion. Blue's breathing eased, his heart slowed back to a familiar beat. Then he became aware of footsteps.

A man walked through the corral yard, raising dust with each step. His head turned toward the darkness of the roofed area and he seemed to recognize Blue. His path changed course, and Blue came to the front of the low-hung roof line. He wanted to meet this man halfway. He had much to explain to him.

"It is good you are up and about. My wife and daughter will be very happy. They have been worried."

This was his host, and once his boss. Blue felt the shame return. It took him a moment, but the words came out, roughened by the panic and the need to know.

"The mare. Did she come in? And the colt. Feel real bad about them."

The raised hand cut him off. “You have asked that question many times these past months. The mare is fine. Carrying another foal to my stallion. And the colt is turned out with the others of his own age. They are well, Señor. So rest your concern.”

In foal. Past months. My God, how long had he been here? Blue found he needed the wall again, needed something solid to lean on and digest the news. Must be coming to fall now; missed the whole damned summer. The boss seemed to be reading his thoughts.

“It is late now, almost October. You have been with us five months almost. The bullet angled from your shoulder blade, passed through you into the ground, but it almost took your life with it. It is a miracle. The doctor believes it was only the unreasonable chill of that night that kept you from bleeding dry.

“It was my daughter who brought you here, and who has kept you alive. It was she and my wife who have done the nursing. Let us both be thankful for their care.”

There was a long pause when there were no words. Blue knew it would take him time to sort out the long months, if ever. But for now, just standing here, feeling the warmth of the late sun sneak under the low roof, was enough for him. He gave his own silent thanks.

Rafael Maldinado watched the young man who had almost lost his life for a horse and an unknown hatred. The insolent blue eyes were sunken deep in the long bony skull; dark shadows rimmed them to give an unholy glow. But the go-to-hell look was still there,

and had been the first time the lids had opened. Thi
one had not yet changed.

"What do you remember? Did you see the killer
There was powder on your shirt, he must have bee
very close.

It was only fragments at first that he could pu
together in words. But the beginning of his descer
into the canyon, the appearance of the smiling mar
brought the day back to Blue with a gut-twistin
spasm of fear. It must have showed on his face, for th
Señor reached out a gentling hand to touch him on th
arm. But Blue shook his head against the kindness an
plodded through the splintered story, exhaustio
slowing his words at the end.

"Guess they was certain I was dead. Kept talkin
over me as if I was nothing. About the Indians
Geronimo. Figured to take the mare's head and put i
on a post to teach you manners about the Indians
Could hear them as if I was someplace else and lis
tening in. Reckon you know what all that means, 'bou
the Indian and all. Didn't figure to please you, findin
that head on a post."

The utter stillness of the man came through to Blue
A complete and rigid silence, the breath barel
entering and leaving the body. The rambling length o
the violent tale changed the man from a quiet an
thoughtful listener to a living statue.

Rafael snorted. It had been a warning, a cruel an
vicious act meant as a warning. To him alone. Bu
there had been a witness left behind, who now gav

im a face that he could put a name to. Vace Yarborugh. And the other one with him must be the heavy ne from Warner's store. Was Charlie Warner in on his? He eased the tightness and turned back to the oung man who had been promised fifty dollars to ride nto this feud, and had almost died from it.

He looked closer. There was a fear that widened the nurky blue eyes, that put the thin back against the dobe wall. Then Rafael looked even closer into the larkening eyes. It was more than fear, it was a deep rembling, a life-stealing tiredness. A fine sweat on the orehead, a heavy pull to the eyelids; this was exhausion stealing back from the weakness of fear.

Rafael supported one arm and turned the boy around o the house. Blue walked back into the welcoming oolness. There was no fear inside. That would wait intil he was stronger, better; then he would ride with he Señor to find the killers. Blue leaned into the trength of the man, and shuddered at the touch of oldness as the door opened.

★ Chapter 8

Her fingers were better suited to other tasks, And here were other chores she far preferred to the lemands of sewing, but a quick glance at Mama's face einforced the necessity that she do this task, and without complaint. There was no easing to the set of ner mother's jaw, no humor in the hazel eyes. Outside here was a special three-year-old that needed gentling, but inside there were shirts and socks and a soft blue flowered dress that needed mending.

"Mama, why do the people in town hate us so?" The words came rushing out of her before she could stop them. And she shuddered at the flare to her mother's eyes. But she did want to know. It had been three months since Papa's last trip to Tucson. Yesterday he had mounted the brown gelding and taken the lead to the pack horses; yet there had been no laughter in him, no eagerness for the visiting. She remembered trips when they all rode in the wagon and stayed two days.

"Celita, there is only nonsense in your words. There is nothing to fear in your father's trip. Child, get on with the mending and leave the worry to those who know. There is no one who hates us, and many who are friends. Your father has business with these people and with our good friends in town."

There was more Celita wanted to say, more questions to ask and hope for the right answers. But slow footsteps across the tiled floor stopped her. A familiar face appeared in the doorway.

"Morning, ma'am. Miss Celita." Blue Mitchell stayed outside the door. After two weeks up and around, he had not lost the embarrassment he felt around the two women who had nursed him. They owned an intimate knowledge of him that rode uneasy.

"Ma'am. Thought to try riding this morning, but I be slow getting to the horses. Your riders are gone now, and I don't want to just help myself. Wanted you to know what I be about."

"Mr. Mitchell, you are not well enough yet. You need . . ."

"Ain't fitting for me to speak up, ma'am, but I best get back to a horse and soon. Been taking up your time long enough now. Need to try myself and get going. Just want you to know I weren't stealing a horse or gear, just going to saddle and ride a spell."

Blue stepped back and dropped his head in a curt nod, then walked away from the mother and daughter. It wasn't getting easier, talking to these women. He stopped to wipe away the sweat gathering at his hairline. Women. Couldn't meet them two pairs of hazel green eyes yet. More willing to take on them big cactus and a pair of rattlers. Blue moved quickly and found blessed freedom in the dusty outside and the heat of the air.

Thoughts and fears went back and forth between mother and daughter quickly, without words. Blue Mitchell was still weak, had spent too long in bed, and not yet gained back the strength lost to the months of fever. He wore out fast, pushing himself each day to exhaustion. The long and homely face showed the strain. Celita's head turned as they heard the soft sounds of his coughing. Already this morning he had come close to his limit. And now he was headed out to ride.

"Go, child. You pick the horse, you ride with him. Trail him if you must, but do not let him go off alone."

Her exit from the room left a mound of blouses, one long sock, and her mother with a gentle smile to ease the ache of her constant worry. The two young ones Caught up in their discovery of each other, enchanted with the new world they had invented for themselves

Ruth looked down at her hands. She remembered her own discovery of that world. Her hands came into focus: nails broken, veins standing out across the tanned backs, skin wrinkled and stained. It had been an instant recognition of Rafael and what he would mean to her. Now it was her daughter's turn.

Even behind those insolent eyes and borderline drawl the boy was courteous in an awkward way, shy and uncertain. As her husband told her, he could be a wild one. Yet around Celita and herself he retreated to mumbled stammering and long silences.

Her hands had a life of their own. Without thought they went back to the details of the mending, leaving Ruth Maldinado with her memories.

"Take the bald-faced sorrel. He's nice and gentle won't give you much trouble."

As soon as she spoke, Celita knew. Twice today she had spoken wrong. She watched red color the long face, saw the odd blue eyes darken. The words, when they finally came, were soft with anger.

"Thanks anyway, missy. I can pick my own mount Even wore out like I am I can ride anything. Ain't nothing can lose me once I hit the saddle."

She let her own anger come full blast. "I picked up the pieces of you once, and don't want to do it again You listen to me this time."

Blue turned away from the girl. Rope in hand, one ɔop hanging from his right hand, coils drooping down is left side, he walked to the horses. Damn her quick nouth, and damn her more for being right. He knew he was watching as he twisted the open end of the ɔpe and let it slip out to catch hold of a big red bay. 'he horse pulled back for an instant, went up, and then ame back to stand quiet. A fighter this one, but a good onest fighter.

Celita climbed the tight weave of the mesquite encing, cursing as always at the hooks and knobs that aught at her clothing. She wanted a good seat for the reworks, and to be close when he hit the dust. Half er mind wanted him punished for going against her rders.

But he was only standing in the center of the pen, ope held loosely in one hand, talking softly to himelf, barely-muttered words she could not hear. She vatched the bay. The horse seemed to be listening, ars tipped forward, eyes settled on the tall and waying young man. It was as if the horse understood.

His fingers tightened on the rope, tugged lightly at he bay gelding, and the horse came forward first with ne step, then three, then stopped for another look, and valked quietly to stand with muzzle touching the oose folds of the white shirt. Blue reached out and troked the searching nose; the bay blew through disended nostrils and Blue's hand cupped the hot air.

She was fascinated. The tall figure turned and valked away. The bay horse followed on a loose line.

Celita slipped from her narrow seat and ran to the small shed that held the ranch gear. She wanted to saddle the yellow mare fast before Blue got away from her.

His eyes adjusted fast in the dimness of the shed, and Blue found his own gear in the corner. The narrow horn and rounded swell were easy to see among the low, split seats and flat horn of the spanish saddles. There was a polish to the old hull, oiled and smooth, even repaired at the torn skirting and cut away strings. He thought to thank the girl, but her head was buried in the belly of the old mare, fighting to pull the cinch another notch. Her stubborn silence kept him quiet. He was building up quite a debt to these people.

The bay had two bucks in him that loosened Blue. But the big horse did not take the advantage. He picked up an easy lope to follow behind the switching tail of the yellow mare. Blue locked hands on the horn and fought for his balance. He couldn't be this weak, this off-center and fighting for air from the two lady's crow hops. His snort of disgust turned to a dry cough that slowed the yellow mare's run. Celita's dusty face came back over the cantle to watch him. He tried to smile, and bent double with a cough.

His pride hated it, but Blue admitted to himself that the walking was easier; he could find enough air at the slower pace without much struggle. The bay jigged for a few steps and then settled. Blue got his breath in two gulps of air, and spoke to the back of the girl's head.

"Now, how about you take me up to where you

ound me. Want to see it sitting from a saddle. Want to now how I got back down here."

The reply was curt; "I can tell you how you arrived lown here, mister. Slung over the seat of that old addle, head buried in the buckskin's belly. That's how 'ou got here. And if I take you back up there today, 'ou'll come down the same way. Only this time for a ertain burial."

She angled the mare across the narrow path. "You isten. You got your way to sitting up on that particular iorse. And maybe you'll be all right. But now you ollow along. There's enough trouble without having o nurse you again. This one time you do what you've een told."

She watched the flare in those heavy blue eyes and tood ready to battle with him. Then the anger died as he saw the weary set to him. And she smiled, to lessen he taste of her words.

"Thought you might like to see some of the stock. The bunch of new weanlings usually graze the day in a small canyon about a half-hour walk from here. It's eally pretty. Papa grains the weanlings each evening o they come back to the ranch, but they always end up n the canyon, and you can't blame them. Anyway, I hought you would like to see them. The chestnut colt's there."

Blue had to see it her way this time. He bit off an angry word and eased himself into the support of the high cantle.

"Yes'm. Sounds good."

There couldn't be any fight to those words. He wa almost wrong. The girl looked back at him queerly, the shook her head as if in anger and swung the yello mare back onto the trail. Blue followed the stiff, s back, and let his mind wander, to feel the heat soakin into him, the loose rhythm of the horse beneath him.

The yellow mare stopped at the first shot. Then series of shots came, carefully spaced as if taking prac tice at a target. Blue had no answer for the question i the girl's eyes. They were silent to listen for the nex shot, then Blue shook his head. Between the narro ridges and piled rocks, he couldn't find the direction c the sounds.

Celita knew. She slapped the yellow mare to a ru and the bay came in a leap that almost left Blue on th ground. A ten-minute scramble and the trail opened t double width. Blue dug in his heels and yelled at th big bay gelding, chasing him past the girl on the fa tering mare.

The pair leaned into the corner and burst into th small canyon. The bay stopped and went high on hi hind legs, squealing in his fright. The yellow mar slammed into the rearing horse, knocking him side ways into the brittle rock wall.

There must have been fifteen weanlings grazin here. Blue counted fast, trying to turn the still-warr flesh into unimportant piles of meat. Most were dow and still, blood circling under their heads or showin dark at their chests. There were three still alive, strug gling with their killing wounds. Blue went automati ılly for the Henry that would be under his leg and ound nothing. He turned to the girl, numbed by what as laid out in front of him and by what he had to do.

She stood at the head of the yellow mare, reins held n both hands, knuckles white with the holding. Tears racked white lines through the fine dust covering her ace, spotting the white collar of her shirt. Blue spoke er name gently, and she turned her head blindly to the ound. She could not answer his question, but slowly ulled the yellow mare sideways, offering the heathed rifle on the off side to him. Blue climbed om the bay and forced the reins into her stiffened ands, then took the light rifle and walked to the center f the carnage.

The three still alive were at the far side of the small raze. One sorrel filly made it to her feet to hold a hind eg off the ground, cannon bone showing through bove the fetlock, blood pouring from the hole down ne white stocking to puddle below the hoof. The filly urned to stare at Blue, then hobbled away until her veight came to the off hind leg. She collapsed, vhining in her pain. Blue aimed and pulled the trigger n one easy move and watched the filly flop over on er side.

A thick sigh came from him. The single shot echoed gainst the rock. Blue heard the muffled cry behind im but could not turn to offer comfort. There was othing he could give until his chore was finished.

The bay colt lay on his side, blood pumping from a ole behind his forearm. As Blue came to the colt, his breathing slowed, then stopped. Blue touched his fir gers to the underside of the throat and felt nothing. H rose and continued his bitter walk.

It was the chestnut colt. The big copper youngste that had plagued Blue for the long miles back in th spring. And whoever had created this slaughter ha known the specialness of the colt. For the wide eye chestnut colt was mutilated, not enough to kill bu enough to make his living a hell and his death a cer tainty.

They must have gone after the colt first, worked o him before the shooting spree. The big youngste would walk up to any man and stick out his nose i curious friendship. Blue choked on the hard breath tha escaped through his teeth.

He'd been skinned out from the shoulders back. Th hide, a glossy red, was tacked to a mesquite bush Small burbly sounds came from the drawn-back lips the wide eyes rolled back into the sockets, the tongu protruded from between the short stubs of teeth. Blu squatted down to the colt and placed a hand gently o the damp neck. The colt was alive, but there was n life left to him. Blue placed the barrel of the rifl behind the ears, stood up, pulled the trigger.

The cry from the girl brought him back. He did no have the luxury of tears for this pain, and she neede him now. The walk back to the neck of the canyon an the waiting girl seemed to take him a long time. It wa hard to breathe; his hand trembled on the blue barrel Whoever planned this had done it well. In, out, an one, with no witness. And his contempt of the Mald-ıados a bloody and vicious act. No one would kill this ʼay for sport.

Celita would not lift her head to look at him. She tood alone, fighting the anger and the tears. Instinct ıade Blue put a hand to her thin shoulder and pull her ɔ him so very gently. Bodies barely touching, she ɜaned her head to his chest and sobbed quietly. His and stayed lightly on the thinness of her back, and lue wondered at the clean smell to her. A fierceness e had never known came over him, and kept him ıotionless as she cried.

lue glanced back at the girl as they rode into the still-ess of the ranch. He had seen the brown gelding at the e rail, sweat dried on his coat, cinch loosened to rest. he two pack horses stood head to tail under the scant hade of the shed roof. It was for her to tell her father; was for Blue to put up the horses and wait. Celita did ot look at him, or warn him to take care, but slid from ıe off side of the yellow mare and went toward the ouse. Alone.

Blue stripped the gear from the horses and dumped , not caring about the heavy puff of dust that rose to over the saddles. He was at his limit now, and he ʼould be needed. The two horses wandered to the ʼater tank, and Blue stayed hunkered down against ıe safety of the thick mud wall. He could wait here or a while. It was a long walk to the house.

Something touched his leg and Blue opened his eyes

to fawn gray pants tucked into black half boots at th
level of his eyes. He struggled to stand, then sank bac
as the soft voice stopped him.

"Just tell me. Were there tracks, what direction
How many riders? Tell me."

Blue found his voice, leaned against the comfort c
the wall to push himself erect. Maldinado's pale fac
came into view.

"Looked to be two riders. One horse needing hin
shoes. Split track. Found these shells." He hande
them to Rafael. "Must have left just before we g
there, fresh manure, fresh blood. Knew the land a
right, knew right where to head up and out. Good ain
Hit each youngster with one shot. Betting the filly wa
last, a hurry up shot 'cause we was coming. But th
colt . . ."

Here he stopped. Something took the rest of hi
breath, and Blue sagged back into the wall. He woul
not look at the darkened face beside him. The voic
finally came so softly that Blue almost thought h
imagined the words.

"I will go and look for the tracks, and the men. W
will find them and we will take care of them. Celita i
with her mother. You will stay here for her."

These were not words to argue with. He watched th
man step to the side of the brown gelding and tug a
the cinch. An old man on a sorrel and the Indian h
knew only as Mickey came from the mesquite corral

Weakness flooded him; relief at not having to clim
on the bay gelding and ride, and anger that there wa

ot more to him. Blue felt the trembling start in his nees, spread to his belly and his chest. Didn't think he ·ould even make it back to the house quite yet, never aind a wild ride back to the bloody canyon.

Chapter 9

: was war. He would take only these two men, the ncient Annuncio and Mickey. If there were tracks iese two would find the trail and keep to it. But afael Maldinado knew who had fired the shots; he ·ould be found in the town by now. Drinking and celbrating his simple victory.

Annuncio rode hunched over in the old military addle. He'd added comfort to it for his old bones by a ouble fold of brightly woven tagging. Body broken nd reshaped by too many hard falls, he still rode out arly and came in late. His dark eyes, disappearing in ie years of wrinkles, missed little. The stubborn idian was willing to walk behind Annuncio, and ogether they could see everything.

It was Annuncio who found the first sign. He pulled p the high-stockinged sorrel to lean over and point at ie one track on the windblown trail. A hind shoe, the oe worn thin to cracking. They rode on, picking up to steady lope. There was one more such print before iey reached the small canyon.

It was Mickey who rode through the formless hapes, Mickey who ignored the great flapping birds s they plodded into flight at his interruption. Rafael found he could not look at the torn piles. Mickey drov his horse up the steep incline of the far wall. There wa the hint of a trail that wound back across the slante wall, twisted, and returned to come out on the rim.

At the wave of his hand, Rafael spoke softly to th old man and they put their horses on the obscured trai There were no words to speak, no thoughts to expose about the death they left behind them.

They knew when the trail was lost. It headed sout into a dry wash, then out over glare rock. White line scarred the gray surface to mark the passing. Then th faint tracks hit the wide valley and joined with other to follow the sooted curve of the railroad.

"Annuncio, you and Mickey ride one on each side c the tracks. Follow them forever. And you will fin where these two riders changed horses or turned back.

Rafael spun the brown gelding and pushed the hors to a run. He did not want to see the faces of the tw men. Common sense made him pull up the brown afte less than a mile. He had chosen in a hurry and now h would pay. Habit made him cinch up the brown whe he had need of a fresh horse. Hurry brought him ou with handgun and rifle and no extra shells, not enoug for the war in his mind. He slapped the sweaty neck c the faithful horse and felt the trembling deep in th animal's heart. There was no choice. He turned to th high safety of the ranch.

The trail dipped back into the narrow wash and u across sharp rock to home. Partway up the far side th gelding lifted his head and snorted. Rafael was ready

Three more strides and they came up onto flat ground. Rafael had his rifle angled across the saddle in front of him, hands cradling it gently.

There were two horses waiting. It was Blue Mitchell on a light bay, holding the line to a long-legged buckskin. Arms crossed on the wide horn, the boy said nothing but he held out the bridle reins to his boss. Their eyes met for an instant, and then the bluish-green ones slid away from the hot anger riding the Señor's face.

It took only moments to pull the gear from the brown and tighten the cinch on the buckskin. Blue kept his silence as the Señor slipped the headstall from the tired brown and sent the horse home. The first strides were a jerky gallop that settled to a trot. Then Rafael mounted and they rode out.

"Gracias." The word came after ten minutes of silent riding, and Blue dipped his head. Maldinado looked back at his silent companion and waved a command to ride up beside him. There was a holster buckled to the narrow hip, butt handle gleaming dully. Rafael's gaze went to the saddlebags tied on behind. They bulged with sharp edged indentations. Shells. There would be a rifle on the far side of the bay, and his own horse would be so equipped, too.

He took another look at this companion of his. The hot blue eyes came back at him. There was still no softening to their insolence. Then Blue spoke and the voice sweetened the temper in the eyes, even with the hoarseness of its sound.

"Got a pistol for you, belt too. The missus said you always carried the Sharps. Got extra shells for that. Thought you would need the fire power when you hit town."

Enough fire power for an army from the heft of the bags. There was more to the boy than temper and talk. The horses, for example. The buckskin was a race horse, high-bred and hot-tempered with a willingness to run. Not a stayer, but one to make the speed. And the bay was no less a horse.

Then he thought of the rider, took note of the slumped shoulders, the quick rise and fall of the lean chest. There was no time for compassion. The boy had chosen to ride with him and he would not turn him back. The boy had made his declaration and Rafael needed the ease with the weapons, the hot temper and the sullen eyes. There were no words that would turn this one back.

"Well done. My friend." Blue's head came up at the words. There was no bite to the sounds, no bitter twist to the meaning. "Annuncio and Mickey have continued along the rail bed but they will find nothing we do not already know. You and I, we will find our answers in the town that does not want us. Perhaps we will find the end to all the answers."

There was a continued silence. Blue shifted his weight gently, seeking for more comfort in pushing back against the support of the cantle. There was a deep tiredness that spooked him, as if he would never know a good horse or a bright day without paying leeply for the pleasure. Damn. There could be no iredness now. He owed the man riding beside him his ife, maybe more.

This was going to be real easy. Better than the shooting gallery they set up in the canyon with those weanlings. Bristol Adderson rubbed one hand deep nto his thick hair and found the right spot. Then he brought the hand down to settle against the trigger guard on the new Remington. It weren't only the Mexican government could get a hold of one of these beauies.

It was just like Vace told him. Here came the mex, riding a fancy stepping, high-headed horse. And, by God, it was Bristol's day all right. Along with the mex came that wet-eared kid, riding right beside the big honcho. Gave him two birds for a target instead of only one.

Adderson grinned. He'd taken enough of that kid up north. The boss telling him to leave the kid be, let him work his own way with the broncs. A baby's way. Then the kid would grin at him and those damnable greeny eyes would invite a good punch. Bristol felt the familiar anger rise in him. He was sure going to like pulling the trigger.

He heard the roan move behind him. And he remembered Vace's words. "You shoot that damned mex right off. He'll be coming right at town and riding with some 'a his men. You get him first and then the others." But Vace didn't know that the wet-nosed kid would be the one riding with the mex. Vace was a smart one all right, knew the gut shooting of the colts would bring the mex in on a hot temper. Didn't plan on the kid, though.

The sore-footed roan shifted nervously, raised his head and fluttered a whinny deep in his throat. Bristo sighted on the whiteness of the fancy shirt and squeezed. It was a pretty sight to see the blood spread across the shirt front, to watch the body lean back and drop hard, disappearing in the confusion of milling horses and rising dust.

He moved the sight of the big gun to look for the kid He fired this time without taking aim and the bullet went wide and low, taking a chunk out of the light bay's hide. He watched the bay spin high and wild in a buck that sent the kid flying. Bristol laughed, then dropped back to his belly to take better aim.

The bay gelding had seen something ahead in the brush. Blue followed the horse's ears and saw the shape of another horse tied beyond a rock. His warning was lost in the boom of the rifle and he felt the shock as Rafael Maldinado spilled backward from the saddle The buckskin jumped sideways and kicked at the body, while the bay spun in response to Blue's dig with the spurs. Blue lost his balance, and then the bay went out from under him in a tremendous buck. The shot blended in his ears with the horse's shrill scream.

Then he was lost in the tangle of dark legs and blurring sand. Blue rolled once and came up against the soaking red of the shirt. His hand reached out for the face of the downed man. There was no doubt, the shot had driven a fist-sized hole through the chest, exposing shattered bone and pink muscle. There was nothing Blue could do.

The bay was down, becoming a blockade from the sniper. The buckskin skittered into Blue, frantic from the blood smell, and kicked at Blue's reaching hand. Blue came up to grab at the horn, letting the horse's spin pull him into the saddle. He drove the horse over the thrashing bay in a straight-up leap that carried them closer to the sniper's rock.

A shadow of a man slid from the brush and mounted the untied horse. Blue dug in deeper with his spurs, then leaned down and pulled the sheathed rifle free. The reins hung loose from the long shanked bit and slapped the buckskin at each stride, driving the horse into a faster run. Ahead of them the roan took laboring strides to get away from the madman coming up fast.

Even running free the buckskin was the better horse, Blue the better rider. There was no chance for Bristol to get away. The heavy man knew that for a fact and took his only chance. He yanked the roan to a halt and half fell from the saddle. Reins still bunched in his fists, he raised the rifle and aimed at the wide chest of the fast-approaching buckskin. He waited one moment longer and his target came closer, until he could not miss. Close enough that the wild blue eyes brought back all the hatred, and made the shot a pleasure.

He knew this man. It was Bristol Adderson. Blue

shot twice from the back of the buckskin, and missed. The buckskin was out of control now, running from panic into certain death. The braided reins swung a his shoulder, hitting him in each stride. He brought Blue straight at the kneeling man, and Blue could do nothing but keep pulling the trigger and wait for the killing shot.

Adderson raised his sights to center on the loose body leaning over the buckskin's shoulders. He lost his nerve and lowered the barrel, pulled the trigger and watched the buckskin horse go down on his knees, plow into the sand with his nose, and flip over to land with his head buckled under the lifeless body.

The Henry flew high and came down barrel first to jam into the sand. The kid went wide and Bristol thought he had gone clear. Then one long leg kept its connection with the stirrup, jerking the kid back to stay with the falling corpse and lie still half-under the dead weight.

Bristol grabbed the sweaty roan and rode. He wasn't going to take any chances at all. He shoved spurs into the stumbling horse and lined out toward Tucson. He'd leave the rest of this one for Vace. The mex was dead, the kid down. That was enough for Bristol.

He crawled out from under the weight of the dead horse. Crawled because he could not stand. He knew that Rafael Maldinado was somewhere behind him and began to retrace the last moments he could remember, quartering the tracks made by the wild running horse, fearful he would lose contact with his man. There were times when the effort was too much and he plowed into the sand to sleep. Then he could come to his hands and knees again and continue the search.

Annuncio saw it first. Something making a ragged line across the ground scattered with brush. Without turning his head, he spoke softly to Mickey, and the Indian put his horse to a lope. Annuncio had already seen the silhouette of a lone horse, standing on three legs, saddle empty. That was not good.

The hand on his shoulder pushed hard into Blue's mind, tried to stop his motion. He leaned into the pressure, butted his head against the leather stockinged legs, but his tormentor would not give way. His arms buckled and Blue fell, rutted sand scouring his chin.

Then that same implacable hand rolled him over, and Blue looked up into the dark face of the Indian. Mickey. Blue began to understand. He sat up on his own, and looked for what should be there. His red-rimmed eyes flashed by the Indian, and the man grunted at the color, a blue clouded storm.

The old man was sitting on the high-stockinged sorrel. Blue could only point; he raised his arm and showed the old man and the Indian where he was. In the dry wash. Blue accepted the strong hand and came to his feet, staggered into the solid bulk of Mickey and steadied himself on wide shoulders. They watched the old man guide the sorrel down into the shallow dip. Mickey walked after him. Blue took a tentative step and found he could follow.

It was not easy to stand and look down at the stilled body. By turning his head, Blue could look back and see the outline of the bay gelding, ground tied by the steaming corpse of the buckskin. The bay must have wandered there to find comfort out of the pain. Mickey rode his gray back and picked up the reins of the bay. The crease across his rump had finished its bleeding and the horse would survive.

Annuncio talked in low murmurs to the Indian. Blue did not want to know. Then Mickey slipped from the flea-bitten gray and gave the reins to him, motioning for him to mount and slide back over the saddle. The body of the Señor was balanced carefully across that saddle, and Mickey mounted the lamed bay. They would take the Señor home to his wife, to his child. Then they would come back with the young man from the north, and they would find the man who had done this. His death would not be fast or pretty.

★ Chapter 10

Charles Evans Warner found it hard to look in the mirror sometimes. He knew too well what he would see: the newly-added lines, the sag to the wide jaw, the downward pull at the thin mouth. There were wrinkles and lines added daily. He took to letting his hair grow, and let his sideburns bush out to a wildness. There was only hatred in the face he saw in the mirror now.

And the only reason he was looking was the load of liquor he was carrying. The quart of trading whiskey had made the rounds as they waited at the small iron gate. Yesterday he had stood in the line as they buried Henry Wallem, and today they had buried Rafael Maldinado at the ranch. And today Charlie Warner had gotten stinking drunk.

He turned too fast, lost his balance, and caught himself on the thick plastered walls. Their feel gave him comfort; not for him and his Rosa the fancy dressing of the wood-framed house and horsehair plaster. Warner snorted and stood straighter in the gloom of he long hallway. Damn fool notion to live in double stories when the heat ate you alive most year 'round. Not for him.

'Course, that he couldn't pay for the luxury of such a monster had no bearing on his disdain. Charlie snorted again and walked the distance from the clatter outside he front door to the quiet of the small courtyard.

A shame, to bury a man such as Rafael Maldinado with only his riders and his family in attendance. The man pulled his weight when this was a frontier town. Damned shame. The tall anglo had been to the funeral; Charlie had seen him standing behind the new widow and her child. Been riding with Rafael when he got shot. And word was spreading that the blond kid might have been the one to bring Maldinado down. Didn't sound likely to Charlie; he saw the trust the missus put n the presence of the boy. Not likely.

Shame came back over him in a wild loop, dropping his head and making Charlie Warner fight for his uneven balance. Rafael Maldinado had been his friend for almost eighteen years, since before he married the pretty lady from the train. And yet Charlie had let the talk and the fancies of new power sway him from his friendship, his obligations, and his pleasures with their family.

Charlie slapped his hand down on the dust-covered foldup top to the piano. Something his wife 'had to have,' some fool thing she never touched but to wave a hand at and brag some on him. He bought it for her, and went near to bankruptcy with her whims. While he let a friend go who was proven strong.

Ruth Maldinado had stood bareheaded by the mounded grave, sunlight picking up the gray in her fine auburn hair. The daughter, Celita, was beside her mother, showing the same strength in her set back and proud head. These were not people who had need of a piano or a flight of stairs and a yard of bleached grass.

The self-pity put him in the need of another drink. He was coming too close to thinking on right and wrong, coming too near the anger that rode him each day in the store. Another bottle would back up the feelings and cork the thoughts. Let him open up the store in the morning and be willing to wait on the few customers. Hell with it, he'd take another drink and open up this afternoon.

"Ma'am. We riding out now. Just wanting to know you be all right alone. This got to be settled now. We wait too long and those tracks get covered over. Mickey, he and Annuncio can follow what's left. Me, I'm going for the ride and to find the big-bellied man did the shooting. Knowed him from Utah. Just wanting to know you're all right for now."

Ruth Maldinado knew what the boy was trying to say. But the harsh, spoken words still hurt. She could see into his face and read his mind. Yesterday, only yesterday, Annuncio had ridden in with the gray horse on a line, the body hanging across the saddle, the boy riding the rump of the tired animal, hands steadying the corpse of her husband in the saddle.

She had not cried. There had been no surprise for her, only a pain deep inside that would not soften with time. Her words had come as comfort to the old Annuncio and the sullen-faced Mickey. The tall blond anglo had kept to his silence long enough to put up the horses, then had fallen into a sleep that brought him to this morning.

The simple burial in the small iron-rimmed piece of ground freed the men. She asked only that they wait until he was buried. Now they could ride and now she would return to the few hours of her private grief. Celita had taken the yellow mare and ridden into her hills. Soon mother and daughter would come back to work the ranch and to live with their pain.

She looked up at the boy. There had been no hesitation in him, no holding back. "Why are you doing this? Why do you ride out with Mickey and the old man? Your debt is canceled and you are free. I have the bill of sale for a horse of your choice, and your gold piece. You have never taken them. Rafael said to wait, that you would come to him. But you are staying to fight for a cause that is not yours. Why?"

She was asking more than he knew. Blue shifted his feet, pulled at a lock of hair sliding past his eye. He didn't have the words that would give her a good answer.

"Ma'am, the Señor. He give me a place, a trust. Don't know how to say it. Figure I got a debt to him that I got to pay." He lost his nerve and shuffled back out of the dark room. The room where he had spent those long months. It was her mourning room now. His voice was loud enough to be heard beyond the thickness of the walls.

"We're riding now, ma'am. Back in a few days."

There was no need for talk among the riders. Mickey led, his flea-bitten gray walking out with long strides. Annuncio covered his back, off to the left and checking for what Mickey might not see. Blue rode farther back and to the right. He checked the ground but did not expect much. It was the two men riding ahead who would find the sign. Blue was the eye in the back of their heads.

The shallow wash and the body of the buckskin were easy; the indentations by the rock that gave the weight and size of the killer were there for anyone to read. It was the wild run back to the limits of the city that was the trouble. Not the trail, for even a day later it was clear, the hoofprints deep and wide-spaced in their speed, straight-lined to the streets of the city. It was the city that would give them the trouble.

Annuncio brought his high-stockinged sorrel up to the red bay of the boy. He knew Mickey's mind and knew that the Indian would not speak his thoughts. It was for him to ask the question. And for the light-haired anglo boy to know the answers.

"You know this man. He is the rider of the roan and the killer. Yet you say he is not the one to blame, that there is someone behind him. We cannot ride into the city and point our gun at his fat face."

"Señor Maldinado gave me a name as we rode yesterday. Vace Yarborough. Said he'd been riding lately with a fat man, fitted Adderson's type 'a friend. We find them in town, do some checking on their horses, whether they been around. Someone'll know something."

The silence that followed set an edge to Blue, but he waited it out. Annuncio took his time thinking over the few words, then looked up at Blue and nodded as if something had been decided. Then the old man pulled back to put his horse alongside Mickey's gray. Blue waited, until Annuncio flicked his hand at him as if to move on a reluctant horse or a neighbor's dog. Guess he wanted Blue to get going. Guess it was left to Blue to make the entrance into town.

There was a swelling in his throat, a high lump that wanted to gag him. There wasn't enough to him to lead good men like these, to have them willing to follow his lead. He wanted to rein his pony a step back to fit in between the two riders. One look at Annuncio told him it couldn't be done. He put the bay to a lope and shortened the distance to town considerably.

He'd never been this far before. Been to a couple of wide-open cow towns up north, been once on the train to Chicago. Rode the box car with two fancy saddle broncs heading to a new city home. He'd been paid well for babysitting them, and lost it in one night with a pretty girl and a fast-talking bottle of whiskey. But he'd never been to Tucson before.

Blue put the wonder aside. He needed to find Yarborough and the fat man that rode with him. The rest of it: the odd angled streets, the wet greenery of the park at the end of the main road, the staggered two-story houses built between the street level adobe buildings of the old town, and the people, Lord, the people. He had to put all that away until there was time.

His head got stiff going from side to side, checking all the people flowing past him, headed in some other direction. Each time he turned, he could see Annuncio to his left, hunched deeper in the split saddle, hand resting protectively on his old rifle. Mickey came into sight from the right, dark face pulled pale, eyes never still, rifle out in the open and crossed over the saddle. One hand was clenched on the handle of a knife.

The words came out of nowhere.

"There's the man. There's the son of a bitch shot Maldinado. With the Indian and the old mex. He's a killer."

Blue hauled on the bay. Mickey's gray jammed into the horse's rump. Annuncio angled the sorrel to stand close and reached for his rifle. It was a short, gray-haired man, belly pushing at his leather vest, mouth wide, words coming out fast and ugly.

"I saw that son of a bitch. Waiting to shoot his own boss. Bet he and the Indian got fancy ideas. Got to keep this town safe. Can't have no killer like that 'un loose here."

Vace Yarborough thought fast. Never would have guessed the kid would ride right into Tucson looking for him. There he was, by God, sitting on a fine bay gelding, riding like he owned the town, with his escort crowding behind him. An Indian, too. Got him.

Geronimo running wild, Crook, Crawford and their men taking chase and finding only ghosts in the empty wind. Word kept coming back about meetings that never took place, talks that turned to dust. The Indian was his key. Vace's tone rose to a high pitch.

"Got hisself a chief for a bodyguard. That's the man, he done in Maldinado."

There were no calm minds to take a stand, to ask the right question. No law to wonder how Vace knew. The high scream of the words brought out a fever in those on the wide street. The three riders became a fearsome group, horses bunched and frantic, riders clothed in buckskin leggings and wide red headbands, rifles clear of the scabbards, held loose and ready to fire into the crowd.

Vace screamed again. Working on the noontime stragglers waking from a whiskey sleep. "Killed a man just outside a town. Killed his own boss, helped by the mex and that damned Indian."

Annuncio never heard the shot that entered his head, tearing out his brain and his life. The old man's body dropped from the comfort of the padded saddle and rolled in the dust under the wild, spinning horses. Vace grabbed a pistol from a man, took aim and shot in haste at the hatless blond head of his enemy. The bullet went past Blue's ear, taking the top off in a stinging scream. The crowd panicked at the explosion of shots, and pushed at each other in a scramble to get away.

Vace didn't want the kid ending up in jail, didn't want the law to hear the contradictions that would come from the kid's mouth. He knew enough to kill Vace in this town. The pistol kicked back in his hand as Vace pulled the trigger without sighting. The erratic aim brought down a thin-faced man wearing the stained apron of a butcher. The man sat in the middle of the chaos and put both hands to his belly. His own blood overlapped the animal stains covering his chest. The feel of its wetness drew a high scream of terror from him.

Vace picked up the scream, howling his addition to the growing crowd. There was no way the kid and the Indian could get out of this now. He shot twice in rapid succession, howled again in pretend pain and gloated over the satisfying results.

Hands reached for the gray's bridle, fingers tore the rifle from Mickey's grasp. It dropped free beneath the horse's front feet, kicked hard enough to splinter the tock and then was jammed under the steps. The bay gelding reared high above the crowd, forelegs dangling over upturned heads. The mass moved back from the menace of the shod hooves, and the hands dropped away from Mickey. Blue balanced the horse and held him in the wavering rear.

Blue spun the bay with his knees, left hand sweeping out to scoop up Mickey in the wide turn. The Indian crambled onto the bay's rump as the horse came down hard. Directly ahead was the low entrance into a store. Behind them on three sides were angry people, earching for weapons, pulling out six-guns and finding the trigger guard. Blue dug in the spurs.

The horse slipped on the dust-scoured bareness of he wooden flooring. Charlie Warner heard the clatter of shod hooves on his downstairs planking. He put down the bottle hard enough to raise dust. The yelling and the shots were nothing new, but this intrusion was an outrage. He came halfway down the stairs, and saw he looming shape of a horse spin past the counter, knocking nails and the new shipment of hinges in a wild splurge of destruction.

He recognized the long blond hair of the rider. And knew the Indian perched half-off the bay's hind end. The bay came to a halt inches from his head; he shrank back, protected by the thickness of the railing. The rider looked hard at Charlie Warner and he knew an nstant fear at the wildness in the odd blue-green eyes. The horse settled, the Indian pulled himself snug to the cantle. And the rider kept his eyes on Charlie, making no move toward the revolver in its holster, shaking hi head when the Indian touched a hand to the sheathe knife.

"No, he's got to give this to us."

Crowds were at the front door, jammed into eac other at the width of the door, reluctant to make th first move into the dimness of the interior. Eager fo their quarry. There was only a moment's time.

Charlie put both hands to the railing and slid hi body underneath. Still holding to the rough wood, h dangled his legs and let go, landing almost on the ches of the bay. The horse only shuddered and raised hi head, beyond anything that could spook him now.

"Quick. Follow me. There's a platform out here, an a road."

Charlie pushed past the horse and found the locke door, slipped the inside bolt and opened it, then ran th length of the stockroom to the double width of th loading door. He could hear the hesitation in the bay' steps as the blond-haired rider pushed through th narrow opening into the confusion of the stacke goods. It took Charlie another moment to slide bac the two bolts of the big doors and open them to th startling brightness of the day outside.

The bay hesitated. Blue patted the sweated neck, an then drove in the spurs to push the horse onto th narrow edge of the platform. Mickey yelled, an eeri whoop that gave the bay the needed courage, and th big horse jumped out from the platform, shod hind fee sliding on the slick wood, knees buckling as the weigh f the two riders slipped forward on the landing.

They were free. Behind him Blue could hear the oices rise, boot heels hitting the planking, words elled in outrage. Mickey slapped the bay hard with he flat handle of his knife, while Blue dug in the spurs emorselessly. The horse came up from the dust and ucked into the narrow street, headed north in a hurry. Ieaded through the proper homes and watered lawns ɔ the safety of the mountains. Blue yelled with each tride, Mickey bounced and flailed at the panicked ıorse with his legs. They were free.

At the front of the small store, now jammed with the ngry yelling of newly-brave men, Vace Yarborough urned to his fat companion. There was a shine to Adderson's face, a sweated fear.

"Bristol, we got trouble. You better find that kid and he Indian, make your shots count this time. You got ourself into a mess this time. And there ain't much I an do about it.

Vace grinned at the confusion in Adderson's round ace. The mex was dead, the kid on the run with the uestion of a killing over him. And Bristol Adderson n his trail. The law in Tucson would not bother with he riders hightailing it for the hills, and the county law vas taken up with the Indian ruckus. What was one nore long rider with a dead mex to his name? Vace iked the odds: the old man dead, the kid and the ndian on the run, and the ranch back up in the mounains run only by women now. It would be the making of him yet.

★ Chapter 11

There was a light at the house. Blue shivered and huddled deeper into the canvas jumper. He thought thi was the desert; not right to be shaking cold at night an steaming sweat in the day. He let the bay come back t a slow walk. Mickey waited behind him in the back o a slanted boulder, to watch their back trail and liste for pursuit. Blue needed only a minute at the ranch t ask a few questions and pick up gear and a mount fo Mickey.

Tucson. The city lights were dim and far off to hi right, but in the clarity of the desert air they could b counted from this high in the mountains. He still di not understand what had happened in the town tw days past. He knew that Annuncio was dead and h and the Indian had escaped; that men had followe them until they reached the confines of a high-walle canyon at the base of the northern mountain range.

Mickey knew the trails. It was he who guided Blu and the bay by short grunts and hand signals. They ha stopped once, to set up an ambush that brought dow none of the riders but took three horses out. It wa enough for the quick-tempered posse to retreat wit double-loaded horses. The dark cut off the posse fro their quarry, and retreat was the only solution.

Away from the angry crowd, the wild yells of hatred Blue put his trust in the silent Indian and followed th winding maze. It brought them across the slopes to th

ʼest. They stayed below the height of the ridge, ʼinding slowly between the fallen rocks, watching the actus claw and thorny bush. Two days working their ʼay in the early light, then holing up until daylight aded. Two hungry days.

Blue suspected that the law would be waiting at the ingle M. He came down to the back side of the ranch, ɔ the spring pens used only for branding. There were wo horses picking over the remains of a hay pile. The ired bay sighed with the release of the cinch and the ush of cool air across his hot back. Blue roped the big un and Maldinado's favored brown. His hands tremled as he rigged the saddle in place. He could feel his ʼhole body begin to shake.

A pebble rattled against another. Blue spun on his eel and went into a crouch, hand carrying the evolver that came up without thought. Then he rose nsteadily, feeling a red flush come up his neck and long his face. Thank the Lord for the near darkness.

"Blue, what happened? We've heard so many sto-ies."

Her voice was sweet to him, the slenderness of her omething he wanted to draw with the tips of his fin-ers.

"I can bring you supplies, a coat, some food. You nd Mickey need more than just horses." She stopped nd the words came with a struggle. "We know about Annuncio. Mama would not let us open the coffin. He s buried up with Papa."

Then the anger came back. "They were here looking

for you. And blaming you for Papa's death. Mama wa very gracious and said we would send word."

There was a long hesitation in the talking. Blue huddled into himself and waited for the condemnation.

"Here." Celita held up a saddlebag, each side thic with necessities. "I have had this ready and waiting fc you to come get the fresh horses. There is a saddle an gear for Mickey on the fence."

How could he have doubted her? She knew hir well, cared for him through the fever days. Blu smiled at his own stupidity as he gently lifted th leather bag from her hand.

It was a relief to have him standing in front of he Celita looked hard at the young anglo with the blon hair growing wild and long, the blaze in the blue-gree eyes cautioned by the hard days. The paleness ha gone, the insolence tempered by reality.

Following the days of worry and the nights o wonder, Celita took the three steps that separated he from Blue. She leaned into his body, head reachin under his chin. There were no words from him, n groping hands or rough kisses. It was enough to stan there, pressed lightly against him, hearing the steadiness of his heart, knowing again the strength in hi body.

Blue was afraid to breathe, afraid that the thudding o his lungs and heart would spook her. It was a sweetness he had never known, a trust that was not part o his life. The grass-fresh smell of her hair, the soft curv that fitted into his hips and leaned against his thighs.

He did not need to be told; he leaned down and put is mouth to the wire sharpness of her hair and pressed ently. She stirred softly and brought a wildness with er movement. Then she lifted her head and stood up n her toes. They touched at the mouth.

Blue backed away suddenly. Celita was alone, eyes ›llowing his retreat. "Blue, there is more you must now. Please wait."

Instinct told him to run; desire and shame kept him ırned away. She was a child still, not yet a grown ›oman. He could not look at her.

"There's a warrant out for you and Mickey. They say ou killed Papa, and they have a witness. There are ıen waiting everywhere for you. There is a reward out nd the law wants you back in Tucson anyway it can et you there. Be careful."

These were sobering facts. Blue came around to look t the girl, to listen to her story.

"They let us have Annuncio, but they promise to ang you, and to butcher Mickey. Everyone is frightned about the Indians. They've left the San Carlo :servation again. It is only Mama and I up here now, nd the few vaqueros who do not have families. The :st have gone back to their homes and their families. 'he whole valley is afraid."

"Miss, get the men to return here, to the ranch, and ring their families. The gardens can grow again next ear. Your pa built a fortress up here and you all will e safer. You'll have your own army."

What he said was of great practicality, but why did

he find it so easy to walk away from her, to talk c ordinary matters? Why did he not watch her face, c touch her hair? Celita twisted her fingers togethe willing them not to reach up and slide along the ridg of bone just below his eyes, or touch the silkiness c the matted yellow hair. The echo in her mind was c his heart, not her own. How could he stand there an not hear the sound?

Blue saw the change in her eyes, felt the warmth i his belly. He needed out of here, quick.

"Thank you, Miss. Obliged for the supplies, and th horses. Be on my way." He choked, spat, and trie again. The words were muted and not enough. "I than you."

It wasn't what she wanted. The supplies and th horses. Over the quiet steps of the two animals, sh spoke her own thoughts.

"I love you, Blue Mitchell. I love you."

The words were the right ones and she was glad the were spoken, even if only to the wind and the hard packed ground. She did not know that Blue Mitchel had stopped walking at her voice and heard what sh said. Words he had never heard before.

He rode blindly into a hand that pulled the red dun t a stop. It was the Indian who looked up at him fror the blackness of the shadowing boulder and grunted a his gringo slowness. Blue's head swiveled at th sound, and saw the dark face. Mickey.

He tugged and brought up the saddled brown, word

:ssly handed the reins to the Indian who was in the addle from the off side. For one moment longer they it in the dark, able to count the clear new stars. There 'as a fresh eagerness to the two horses, a drive in iem to move on.

Mickey pushed two blunt-tipped fingers into Blue's rm and brought his hand to his mouth, circling his pen lips to mimic eating. A smile crossed Blue's face t the gesture. As they rode they poked into the stuffed ags to find hard biscuits, beef jerky, salt bacon, and offee grounds. On top there was a treat: a tin of ooled stew, sweet with wild onion and carrot greens. ilue used his fingers to shovel the thick liquid into his iouth, and watched as Mickey worked his own meal 'ith quick hands. There was a grin in the dark eyes, a mile blurred by the eating motions. Blue nodded. Iothing had ever tasted better to him, either.

With no words, there was a transfer between the ien. Mickey took the brown off the narrow path and et the horse to climbing up the impossibility of jum-led rock and cactus. Blue followed; it was Mickey's how now. The horses scrambled around the bigger ɔcks, stopped to scent the thin trail, settled on their ocks, and picked front legs over sharp ledges, drop-ing down carefully to new ground.

The food settled into an urge to sleep. The edge harpened by two days of running was wiped out by ieir full bellies. Blue's head nodded as he dropped ito moments of sleep only to be brought awake by a imp from the dun horse, then lulled back into sleep by a few strides on level trail. Mickey knew whe they were headed, even in the darkness.

Blue jerked awake from a hand reaching for h elbow. He looked into the grinning face of the India and felt the heat color his face. They were standing i a small piece of flat ground, sheltered from invadin eyes by overhanging rock. Mickey slid from th brown, knelt to the ground with the reins tied to h wrist, and lay down with closed eyes.

Blue followed Mickey's lead, but took time to loo where they were. There was only room for the tw horses. No graze, no water, no sweet brush for th horses to chew. Only hard ground hidden by leanin walls. A safe place for a good sleep. As he stretche out on the comfort of the rocky floor, Blue watched th stars blacken out, obscured by the tip of the rock ledg He thought to work on what to do next, and was aslee before the thoughts came together.

Where would those two go with the whole valley aft them? Celita stayed too long at the back corra watching the spot where Blue had disappeared leadin the extra horse. She mourned for her father, grieve with her mother, and wanted to ride with the man wh was supposed to be the killer.

She walked easily in the blackness, knowing th ground under he feet well enough to move blin folded. She would stay with Mama for now, and the would call in the vaqueros and their families to mak up a private army. The blue jacket army was on th nove against the Indians, and revenge would be taken. here were already stories of silent raids and murered clans.

She almost let her thoughts go back to the tall anglo ding the mountains tonight, but forced her mind to tay with the immediate troubles that she could deal vith. It would have to be her faith that stayed with im, not her thoughts, or her body.

here was little of comfort through the short days of vinter. Mickey kept them moving constantly, finding ideaways deep in the mountains, coming out to find etter graze or to search for game. Blue followed the ndian blindly, and grew used to the sight of the quare-shouldered back and banded black hair. He ccepted the leadership without question.

It was existence now. Running from constant threat, iding from any sign that did not fit in their narrow vorld. There were a few times they crossed the lmost-hidden track of a long trail. Mickey would heck back to Blue and point out the thin ribbon that ollowed to where the mountains smoothed out into ne flatlands.

Blue had no interest in whatever importance this trail ad for Mickey. He urged his dun across the faint track nd back up into the safety of the mountains. He did ot wait for the Indian to catch up.

★ Chapter 12

There was a change in the air. The days were longe colder, with periods of rain that battered their bodie soaked into the horsehair padding under the saddle split the threading on boots and clothing. Blue shi ered in the wet and rode in constant misery. The rai seemed to run off Mickey's shoulders and down th outside of his high-topped moccasins.

A fire took forever to light. Mickey chose a goo site, under a slab of rock, but the water-soaked woo did not burn. Mickey watched the young man wh rode with him, and felt a worry build in him. Fac drawn, shoulders high, shaking with the bitter we ness, the boy moved head down and silent. A dı cough started, and there was a flush of red high c each cheek.

There would have been lung damage in the bull that had almost taken the young one's life. And th narrow-brimmed hat, the threadbare shirt, and wo canvas jumper did not offer the needed protectio Without fire, food, and warm clothing, this one woul sicken again and die. It was for Mickey to plan so th did not happen. It was for the young señorita that th gringo must live.

The fire caught this time, the warmth feeble in th damp of the night. Mickey risked broadcasting the camp and roasted a small hare he trapped. The me was good, hot and greasy. Not enough to put fles ack on the young one, but enough to warm the soul ıd almost fill the belly.

He boiled the bones and the innards in a small air-ght and forced Blue to gag down the fat-soaked quor. It would be enough for this night, but there ıust be more, and greater, warmth. They would have risk a return to the ranch.

Routine had been distilled to bare existence. Blue ıimicked the Indian's daily chores, pulled grasses for ıe dun and the brown, made snares from braided ɔrsehair thongs, saddled and rode behind the brown ɘlding, and dismounted and held the horses while Iickey disappeared. It was a passive series of days ith no need or desire between the two men to speak.

This morning was no different, except that Mickey atched the gringo with speculating eyes, counting ıe slowness of his work around the horses, the stiff-ɘss as he packed and tied his gear to the saddle, icked clean the bones of the camp, and stood to ıount. It took him three tries to get his boot in the irrup. And there was the coughing, more frequent, ith a ragged dryness that would double the boy with s draining power.

Blue paid no mind to where the horses put their feet, here Mickey would choose to ride. He had come to smallness in his days, where it was his work to draw r in and push it out from his lungs, where the heat in ıs body warred with the coolness of the winter air, ıen turned on him to bring a chill that shook him in ıe saddle. The dun knew to walk in the brown gelding's footsteps, and there was no need for Blue t put a hand to the knotted reins.

This day the dun walked quietly, sometimes slowin when his rider bent double to one side of the hor shifting weight to threaten the dun's footing. So it wa the brown who first sensed the difference, who quick ened his step in anticipation. This was home rang The brown horse jigged, tossing his head and ignorin Mickey's slap on the side of the neck. This was hom range.

Blue lurched forward in the saddle and almost sli off as the big dun horse gave a half buck. Mickey raised hand brought both horses to a halt. Blue leane over and gagged at the constriction in his chest, th bitterness rising into his mouth. He spat and looke away from the bloody mixture that slid off the shin circle of the flat-sided cactus.

The horses stood sprawling downhill, front leg propped on a tumble of rock washed free by the wint rains, hindquarters uphill. Beyond the bottom of th wash and behind a small plateau was the Single N hacienda, the home ranch. Mickey's head turned sid to side. There was a single gunshot, softened by th drone of the rain. The shot was doubled, then th sounds blossomed into a constant volley.

Mickey lifted the brown into a sliding run. He di not look back; he knew that Blue would follow th sounds, hugging himself to the big dun, riding for th life of those at the ranch. They hit the flat ground at gallop. The brown put his head down and squeale ith the pleasure, letting out a wild buck that Mickey ok with a sliding grace. Blue dug in spurs to the dun; ıe buck and he would be gone. The horse put his ɔse out and ran.

Even above the wind at their ears and the staccato ring, they could hear the wild cries. They did not ɜed the sound to know: Indians. Raiding the ranch ıd finding two women. There was a difference in the ɔunds, a deepness to the boom of the Sharps, a ɔllow lightness to the quick action of the Winches-rs.

Mickey pulled to a sliding stop; the dun slammed to the brown in his own effort. The Indian was off ith rifle in hand and on one knee before Blue slipped s feet from the stirrups and came down the off side the dun. He brought the Henry with him, steadied e sight with his elbow on a bent knee, and found mself a target in the back. He sighted high up, ɜtween the shoulder blades. He had to blink rapidly keep the moisture from his eyes.

Then Mickey pulled the trigger, Blue only a beat ɜhind him. They were close enough to see the blood mp from the widening hole in the target's back. Blue ɔughed twice and spat, then fired again. The Indians ere up and gone from the new attack, quick to find eir tied horses and spread down the hillside in stag-ɜred retreat. These were not odds to their liking.

Blue quit firing first, eyes blurring from the rain. He ɜnt double and dropped the Henry into the new red ud. The coughing blocked out the silence of the

rifles for him, and the cheering from the house. H
only knew the fury in his chest, and the bitterness th
wanted to choke him down.

It was Mickey that lifted him to stand, turned him
the dun and hoisted him partway to the stirrups. H
picked up the reins from both horses and started dow
to the ranch. Blue wrapped his hands around the ho
and rode against the sway of the walk. It was all h
could do.

"Mickey. And Blue. You've come back to us."

It was a sweet sound. Blue's head came up, his hanc
relaxed their grip on the horn. Mickey stopped h
walk and pushed the single rein into Blue's fist. Th
gesture brought a smile to Blue that turned into a dee
ening cough.

"Get down, come in the house, and get warm. W
will take care of the horses. Come in, there is so muc
to talk of." That was a different voice, carrying
reserved warmth that Blue could understand. H
nodded down at the familiar face of the Señora Mal
inado and accepted her invitation.

They came into the house to a welcoming of men ar
women, small children in long-tailed shirts, and infan
still crying from the harshness of the short-lived battl
Celita was waiting for Blue, to put a woolen blank
around his shoulders and tuck the ends under his arm
wrapping him in the welcomed warmth.

Blue kept walking, knowing what she was doing b
with no strength left to smile and thank her. His ste
carried him in the familiar pattern, under the low lint

of the big room door and to the right to the short passage that brought him against the half door of the small room. There were children playing in there, on the floor, tears staining their baby-soft faces.

They did not matter; he fumbled at the latch and accepted her help. The bed was there, covered with a green striped blanket and a multitude of straw dolls. She reached the bed before him and wiped the blanket clean. Blue dropped his shoulder and leaned in a roll that eased him on the bed, found the softness of the feather stuffed pillow, and instantly was asleep.

Celita pulled the blanket over his feet, not caring about the red mud that would crack and dry, that would stain the fine woolen blanket and white muslin sheets. She smiled down at the sleeping man, and leaned to kiss him.

A child giggled behind her hands, and whispered to her companion. The room burst into laughter as Celita herded the children out. She enjoyed their pleasure, for it matched her own. She followed the children in to hear the voices of the grownups as they talked.

"Mickey, they came about forty minutes ago. We think there were ten. They were not with Geronimo, but were led by Ulzana. Julio has seen him before. This is our first time for such a raid. We are thankful that the families came here to live, and that you and Blue were enough to drive them off.

"But what about you being here? It still is not safe. He is wanted for my husband's death. And you also. They will not listen to me, they will not accept my word that he is one of us, and that you are our family. They will not come here in the rain, but when it ends you must ride on. We will put together supplies for you. But for tonight, we will have our own fiesta."

The room was cleared after the long meal was finished. Estaban brought out the guitar, Julio found a fiddle of the Señor's, and they put their music together. Even the children danced, hugging each other in their excitement, enjoying this as if it were Christmas again.

Mickey danced, whirling like a madman with a round and smiling woman named Esperanza. Ruth Maldinado sat alone, hands clapping with the rhythm, eyes sparkling with the tears she could not show. She did not look for her daughter; no one did. They all knew the Señorita would be gone for the night. Sitting at the bedside of the blond-haired gringo child.

Two days. He slept two days. All he remembered were gunshots and mud. And the endless rain. The soft brush of Celita's hair as she leaned over to touch his face. That was the best memory.

It was Mickey who brought the outside world back to Blue. He came in the small room carrying a canvas warbag, top open and half-full. He set it down hard, pushed it with his foot toward Blue, and grinned a wild, split-tooth grin. A quick circle of his hands let Blue know they were to ride out this evening, that they would use the darkness to cover their leaving. He had forgotten the existence of the outside world, and for a moment hated Mickey for reminding him.

He would not look at the odd green bag. If he did, hen he would have to accept leaving. Instead, Blue tretched out on the comforting sag of the bed. This vas the first place he ever belonged, and now a lamned Indian was making certain he left. God, he ated Mickey. Blue closed his eyes against the crazi-ess of his thoughts and went back to sleep.

Something gentle brought him back. A hand stroking is chest, a line of warmth stretching from his shoulder o just above his ankle, the give and take of a bit of soft ir on the outside fold of his ear. Blue knew better than o open his eyes. The gentleness might leave him tranded and alone again.

He rolled halfway in the bed, pulling his left arm bove his head to make room for the mass of black air, the face full of invisible freckles. His body shied way from the roundness of the flesh pressing into his hest, the wide heat touching at his waist. Then nstinct picked up his free hand and let it drift from the angle of the wire hair, along the pointed hardness of he shoulder, to the dropped curve that ended in an brupt rise of soft flesh.

God, she was beautiful. And trusting. Blue had had a voman, a hard, brass colored woman, who had drawn im into her and stayed flaccid under his thrusts. She nd the whiskey had taken his boyhood and his first noney.

Celita was different, special, and willing to place erself up against him, take him as he wanted. Blue uzzled into the darkness of the black hair and touched her forehead with his lips. A quiet sigh came from one of them, or both. He felt the softness of her eyelids with his mouth, the salty taste of her tears, the short strokes of hair that guarded her eyes.

His hand came up from her hip to follow the firmness of her back and hold to the boniness of her shoulder and pull her closer. Closer than he believed anyone could get.

They were gone by nightfall. Blue did not look back and Mickey did not wait. There was only the shadow of the Señora Maldinado to watch them as they rode back into the mountains.

It took a time of endless riding, of following Mickey's back deeper into the hills. Blue shrugged into the warmth of the slicker and blinded himself to the world. Mickey did not push; he rode the brown and found hidden campsites. Rabbits were plentiful, and the dried beans and jerky packed in the warbag would feed them a long time. He could wait for the anglo to make up his mind.

"God damn it. I ain't sitting here no longer. This is a fool's way, Mickey. A damn fool's way."

Two heads came up, strings of grass hanging from slack lips. There had been no words spoken for a long time. Mickey did not turn his head. He had known for several days that there would be an explosion coming, and smiled at the growing volley of the sound.

"The Señor knew the man, name of Vace Yarborough. That's the son of a bitch put the law on us and lid all the yelling. Comes to me, I ride into town, we lo some working on my hair, darken me some, put a nat on and some different clothes and maybe I can get n. Alone."

Mickey's grin widened; the young gringo continued: 'Ain't got much of a plan. But I got to do something. Got to find out. Think we can get me looking like somebody else? And you quit that god-awful grinning. We got to get me into that town."

Mickey looked at the anglo, noted what the months nad done. A layering of muscle over bone, hands quick and confident, movements no longer awkward but of one piece. The face had grown and settled into its promise. The eyes no longer held the angry look of rouble, but carried a calm and steady promise. It was this one's time.

"Good. We start." Blue's head came up at the deep sound to the words. Mickey grinned, and held out his nand.

★ Chapter 13

The bottle slammed down hard on the long counter, and brought a foul oath from Vace Yarborough. Other neads turned, other hands went to unfamiliar guns strapped to shiny pant legs. Bristol Adderson paid no attention; he wanted another bottle, and damned fast. His last coin, a silver dollar, hit the bar top and spun in a short circle. Before it fell, the barkeep slid it into his apron pocket and put down the whiskey glass.

Vace wiped his hand across his mouth and then or his pants. Folks were sure nervous enough in thi: town. Word just come in that Captain Crawford's body been gotten out of Mexico, and them Indians had rur off after making promises of peace with Crook Enough to make anyone a jumping idiot. Even hac trains ready to take the worst of the lot back east Almost seventy-five of them savages. Good plan, bu it failed, and had the local boys jumping at a rabbit' sneeze.

Word had gotten out; the 'Ring' was getting smug didn't want the peace that would take the army away Some talked about their sending a whiskey drumme down to spook the Indians with his talk. While some folks lost their homes and their lives, others brought ir dollars from the army contracts.

Well, Vace hadn't got his dollar share yet. He'd beer up with a few of the men supposed to be in this Ring and got nowheres. Old Ernst Steinkellner was talked tc be in this, with his fancy store full of pricey goods. Bu the ugly little bastard had only given Vace a few words of nasty-sounding English. Sounded more like a mouthful of dirty socks. The old bugger had callec him crazy and turned him out of his establishment. Bu Vace, he was too smart to give up that easy. Word was out about him now, and he knew the 'Ring' was waiting for him to find the right man to step up to. The first move was his to make.

He elbowed Adderson in the ribs, and the heavy mar swallowed his liquor and choked down a cough. The blank face swung around, anger sharpening the fuzzy edges. Vace never gave him a chance.

"You finish up there, Bristol, and give me a drink of hat. We got to find the quartermaster supplying the roops. Out to the Fort. He's the son who knows. By God, I be getting old not to think on this before."

Vace shoved Adderson's reaching hand aside and brought the smudged glass to his mouth to drink down he remains of the whiskey, tasting the bitter sharpness o the reservation liquor. By God, he was right this ime. Hit out to the south where them soldier boys was railing, and talk to the supplier. So damned simple.

He left the big dun horse with Mickey. Too obvious an animal for him to keep, too easy a brand to read and remember. Blue knew he stood above the average man down here, but he and Mickey had done some practical magic up in the hills. Root dye darkened his hair, which they hacked short and covered with a wide hat; ittle dye was needed for his face and hands, stained by he new sun of the spring days.

But most of all, Blue no longer looked up. He walked with a proper humility that he put on with the oose shirt, pants, and high-laced moccasins. Mickey figured this one out. Blue had to learn to go small in his mind, head tilted, eyes cast down, staying deep inside, where he kept the child hidden. There was no place in the charade for anger or defiance. It was abject surrender for now.

Walking through the crowds would never come easy,

but Blue found a freedom in no one looking at him. He could stand against a post and watch, his gaze sullen and withdrawn, his eyes hidden by the tilt of his hat, and no one saw him. He stood at the edge of a gathering crowd, pushing close to a column outside Charlie Warner's almost barren store, to read a printed bulletin.

One man emerged from the crowd and pulled down the paper. His voice came out strong over the listening men.

"Dated April 6, 1886: Crook relieved of command. General Nelson Miles to conduct further chase and capture of all renegade Indians. Crawford's body on its way back to Nebraska. Geronimo and his band in the Sonora hills. Seventy-five Indians to be shipped back east on special train."

The crowd cheered, more men wandered over to join the celebration. Now there would be a finish to the Indian troubles, and a peaceable man could go about his business without fear of his home or his scalp. The notice meant little to Blue, except for the safety it meant to Celita and her mother. He moved away slowly.

He made himself count the steps past Warner's store. There could be no purpose to his walk, no sense that he was going to a certain place. Blue felt all the eyes watching him, calculating his intentions and his value.

He made it past the doorway to the end of the street and stepped into an alley to lean up against the wall and find his breath. He checked the street behind him, then looked into the length of the alley. White hand bills covered the opposite wall, well-framed against the tan of the new wood boards.

His eyes drifted past the startling white squares, then came back in a hurry. The first instinct was to push away from his support and hurry to check what he saw. Mickey's words stuck with him: "Move slow, easy. No hurry."

Blue crossed the narrow strip of alley. No one would know the racing inside him as he came closer to the wall and read his own name and description from the frayed reader. Here was the listing of the formal charges against him and the $50 reward. His life wasn't worth much to these merchants, nor his supposed killing of an old friend.

"Adderson, you damned fool. Drop that bottle and it's the last whiskey for a long time."

Blue wanted to drop and spin, find the revolver that wasn't at the tip of his fingers. He leaned into the wall, loosened the pain in his shoulders, dropped his head, and went for an imaginary itch at his ear. His arm angled across his face, but he could see the shadows as the two men lurched past him. They never looked at the tall greaser getting at the louse biting him.

Adderson stumbled at the corner near Margeson's Butcher Shop, closed due to the death of its owner. The sharp elbow that dug into his middle went deep, and made him lose the bottle neck. Yarborough's two hands were cupped and waiting for it before Bristol could complain.

Then they disappeared, to leave Blue shaking with a

coupling of anger and fear. He walked slowly, stayed a good distance. These two were headed someplace tonight. He had no plan but to take Vace out of Tucson to where he and Mickey could get the truth from the man. Bristol Adderson was a complication.

Blue shook his head. Adderson be damned. He couldn't take two men alone. It was Adderson who did the killing but it was Yarborough who sat on the horse and did the smiling. Bristol pulled the trigger, but Vace Yarborough did the thinking. Adderson would have to wait for now. Blue would have his man.

He watched the two weave a crooked line to the far livery barn. Blue had nothing but a sheathed knife, and in the next few minutes he had to take Yarborough free of the drunken Adderson and the volatile town.

He walked closer, almost on tiptoes, hand clenched white around the handle of the knife that Mickey gave him. The stable door swung open. The riders were highlighted for a short time as their fresh horses circled, heads back against restraining hands. Blue could hear the fury in Yarborough's voice as the man struck out with one hand. The slap against Adderson's flesh spooked the range horses as they pushed their way into the street.

Now or never. Blue stumbled into the light chestnut that Vace rode. His lurch caught the horse at the point of shoulder, putting the animal far enough off to loosen the rider. Yarborough's face came around to peer at the crouched figure in front of his bronc.

"You stinking greaser. Get the hell out of my way."

Blue's arms came up to hide his back from the lash of the split end reins. His erratic movements set off the pale buckskin Adderson rode. The horse spun in fright, and Blue heard more cursing as he pushed into the chestnut again, almost unseating Yarborough. Vace's temper busted loose.

The man pulled up one boot from the wide stirrup and lifted the leg, angling toward the crouching man. He lifted high, then jammed the boot down, raking the roweled spur across the exposed back. A deep groan from the covered head was his reward, and Yarborough grinned. He whirled the chestnut around the cowering man, pulling the other leg free for sport. Adderson hauled in the fractious buckskin and watched, then slapped his horse forward, swinging his feet free from the stirrups. He liked the new game.

Blue waited. He took the next spurring with a deeper groan that did not have to be forced. The line of pain brought sparks from his eyes. Head twisted under his arm, he could see Adderson's raised foot, tarnished spur headed for his face.

It was simple to grab the foot and turn it, putting all the anger into the bucking move that sent Adderson over the off side of his horse. The buckskin panicked at the flopping body, and one shod hoof clipped Bristol's head. He landed in a stilled heap.

Yarborough saw the abrupt dismount and laughed. Then he came around to stare at the tall man who now held the buckskin. He started his threat, then choked on it. Something was wrong. The man was staring up at him, eyes clear and wide, head thrown back. A smile was growing on the dark face to show a line of white teeth. Vace gagged at his sudden knowledge.

"Son of a bitch, it can't be you."

It was that anglo kid greased up to be a mex. But what the hell was he doing in town? At the livery stable? In front of the horses? Long fingers wound into the cheekpiece of the chestnut's bridle, and Vace felt the horse being pulled closer.

It was something his liquored mind had to deal with. Standing there in the middle of the damned street as if the town weren't looking for him, as if there weren't posters carrying his picture stapled up all over the damned territory. Vace opened his mouth to cry out, and found a sharp bite touching between his ribs. His hands tightened on the reins, his boots touched the horse's tender sides. The chestnut felt the signals and stepped deeper into the tall man that held the bridle.

"You move that horse one inch and you'll be needing new lungs. Blade's well sharpened, you won't even know it's gone in. Settle that horse."

It took effort to move his spurs from the heaving sides, to make his hands ease their grip on the leathers. Vace could feel the lightest tickle as something warm ran down his ribs inside his shirt. The son of a bitch had drawn blood on him. He took to breathing shallow, let his feet hang loose, then wrapped the reins around the horn and put his hands down, one on each thigh. He wasn't going to do nothing to move this horse around.

Blue nodded his approval, and Vace took the risk of a long breath. Bad mistake. The knife bit in again, reminded him. He went back to breathing short sighs, and watched the tall man beside him. It was whatever this bastard wanted right now.

Careful not to lose the tension of the blade between the ribs, Blue edged the chestnut around, pushing into the horse's shoulder with his elbow, bumping the head with his hand on the long shank of the curb. He stopped the cautious circle. There was the scraping sound of footsteps coming behind him. He could hear a gasp as Vace inhaled a short breath.

It was someone who walked with erratic steps, someone who stopped and cleared his throat, taking too long before he asked his question. Yarborough got smart and spoke up first.

"S'all right, Willy. Bristol got hisself kicked, got drunk and fell down and his damned horse kicked him. This fellow here is going to pick the bastard up and rehorse him. Now get the hell out of here."

Vace choked on the lightness in his voice, the scratching in his throat. The words came hollow and false. Blue tightened his grip on the bridle, dug the tip of the blade in deeper, almost to where the metal wanted to slide into the warm flesh on its own. Blue had to hold back on the handle. Vace gasped and one hand came to his side, brushed lightly against Blue's knuckled fist. Then both men were frozen in their separate worlds. It was up to the drunk, who stood there wide-mouthed and spraddle-legged.

Willy Bodwell never did like Vace Yarborough. Drank too much of other folk's liquor, faded out when the buying came 'round to him. And Adderson, good place for him lying out flat in the dust with a horse shuffling around him. Maybe the horse would take another chunk out of the son and there'd be less of Adderson to cart off.

Willy Bodwell liked to mind his own business, and he went by the pale face of Vace Yarborough and the big mound of Bristol Adderson and never thought anything more about them.

Blue dropped to his knee and reached for the pistol half-out of Adderson's holster. He had the gun in hand and was back at Yarborough's side before the man found the stirrups and thought about his own handgun. The knife slipped back into its sheath, and Blue rolled easily in the saddle of the buckskin. One hand cradled the pistol, aimed it at Vace's widespread belly. He pushed the horse into the chestnut's flank, put the gun deep into Yarborough's ribs, and nudged both horses into a measured walk.

"You ride quiet now, keep your mouth shut, and I won't blow you apart."

He turned the chestnut with his toe stuck into the shoulder to force the horse down the short alley and beyond the north end of town. Finally, he allowed the horses to move up into a lope. He stayed one stride behind, crowding the chestnut, pushing Yarborough into a panic.

"That horse gets one more stride beyond me and a

bullet'll find the spot between your shoulders nice and clean. You made me a murderer, now you can be killed. You want to live longer, you ride with me."

They made a wide loop, and halted briefly when the horses snorted their concern at the stream crossing. Vace cursed and thought of the day when he and Bristol had been out here, hiding in the brush, waiting for Maldinado.

Blue let the horses stop midstream to drink, and Vace suffered the hollow circle of the gun barrel in the flaring puncture made by the knife. He winced at the pain, then quieted.

"Just my way of letting you know. Just getting started. I read you, Yarborough. See your face every time I close my eyes. This is only the beginning."

★ Chapter 14

They did some fast scrambling and high climbing. Vace waited a long time, then gave up and let the horse carry him. Out in these foothills you couldn't run a horse, and Mitchell rode too close behind him, not allowing him the chance to run out. Vace figured it best to ride this one out and count his chances later.

The ground leveled out, the trail narrowed almost to a point, and Vace let his eyes close, his back slump into the horse. He knew Mitchell would get no sleep, and his own dozing gave him the beginnings of an edge. His head nodded in time with the four-beat step, and Yarborough slept.

There were three of them. Black hair greased to a shine, pulled into wrapped tails that hung along each side of their faces. Store-bought shirts, leather leggings, worked moccasins. Three faces that carried an evil in them. Vace started out of his sleep and looked back at Blue Mitchell. A wide grin split the hated face, lit into the wild sea-blue eyes, and sent a shiver down Vace's spine. Then his captor threw the pistol with an easy twist and one Indian picked it out of the air.

"You mine now. You will tell of what you did to the Señor. And you will tell true. These are my brothers. They have come to help."

Blue stood at the head of the chestnut and watched the effect Mickey's words had on the prisoner. Face blanched white, eyes wide, then shut against the fear. Blue turned away. It was the only path to choose, but he did not have to like it.

They pulled Yarborough from the saddle, the three men handling him as if he were nothing but a feed sack. Shoulders bouncing on the ground, he was dragged beyond the small fire, and propped backside to a rock.

They had talked of this. Of the need to pry from the gray haired man his reasons and names, dates; something that would stand up to the law. They would find the words in him, then have him repeat them to a witness willing to listen and to sign. It could take days, or hours. Time meant nothing in the mountains.

Blue shut his eyes. One hour with no sounds to tear at him. He came awake at the first whimper. Vace arborough stood tied to a rock, arms pulled wide to mbrace the hardness, legs wrapped at the ankles, erked tight under the rock edges, and tied firmly to a take. He stood naked, his body shaking in the cold efore the sun. Fat jiggling at his belly, genitals hrunken and pulled up from the bitter air. The vhimper came from him in a steady flow, as his head olled from side to side across the roughness of the oulder.

The Indians sat on their haunches in front of him, not ooking up at him but talking to each other in a quick uccession of words and hands. Each held a knife, ousin to the one still sheathed at Blue's side. While he vatched, one Indian brought his knife up to poke ently at the flesh hanging above Vace's knee. The mall cry gave him much pleasure, and he grinned at is brothers, moving the knife in a small circle into the oose flesh. A bead of blood appeared.

Another hand came up, holding its own knife, inding its own soft spot on the pale body. A new ound, a choking cry, greeted this touch of the knife. The hand dropped back before the knife tip left its loody mark. There was a long silence. Blue rolled rom his blanket and walked past the three, working at naking no big deal about not looking at the prisoner. Yarborough choked over the name, then called out:

"Mitchell, you tell them to stop. I ain't . . ." Blue did not look at him, but sank to his heels and reached for he small pot bubbling over the banked fire. Hot offee, the way to wake up and find the new day. Even without sunrise. He poured his cup full, put the pc back into the coals, and brought the steaming liquid t his face. A wonder. Both hands cupped for warmth, h tipped the coffee and took his first sip. Sighec coughed against the releasing heat, and took anothe sip. He could feel the eyes watching him.

It was Mickey's turn. His jab was stronger, his ain higher, closer. He found a muscle and traced its narrov line of red along the inside of the thigh, following th slack line that went higher into the groin. Yarboroug tried the impossible, to pull himself away from th sharpness of the knife, the line of its attack. He coul feel the honed point prick at his testicles, an screamed.

Blue bit down hard on his lip, wrapped his finger tighter around the tin cup. Anything not to let hi anguish show. He felt the memory of the six gun in hi hand meeting the swinging head, taking out the jellie mixture of the eye. His stomach turned over hard, an he choked on bile.

Then he walked carefully between Mickey and hi brothers to stare in Yarborough's face. Blue took a bi gulp of the cooling coffee, sighed in contentment, an swallowed. He waved the heat of the cup acros Yarborough's face, not offering the teasing liquid, bu letting the aroma heighten the rawness of the day an savagery of the three men who squatted below him looking up at the hanging swell of his belly and th vulnerability of his manhood.

"They ain't done nothing to you yet, Vace. Anc

von't do nothing if you speak up. Got to give us the ight words and put them down on paper. Then we get hem signed. Real simple. Just want to clear my ıame."

There was a time of silence. Blue looked past the amp to the beginning shine of the sun, picking its way ıp the side of the mountain. Lines of light caught the netals imbedded in the rocks, colors broke into the lullness of the gray sky.

"Going to be a pretty day, Vace. Enjoy it. Could be our last one. Take a good look."

Blue gave him no time but walked away, stopped to efill his cup, and found a soft spot next to a smooth-haped rock. He nodded to Mickey, and the Indian rought his knife up, very slowly retracting the muscle ıp into the groin. The flesh puckered and twitched vith its own life, and Vace howled. The Indian showed ıothing as he found the tiny point of blood he had lrawn before, and put the sharp tip to the same spot, going deeper this time, cutting through the hairy outer covering of the skin, touching the round shape inside.

The howl grew. Eyes wild, mouth open to an impos-ible size, the sound came from Vace in increasing vaves. Tears flowed down his face and his head hrashed from side to side, hitting the rock with a soft ınd rhythmic thudding.

Blue let the sounds go over him. It was Maldinado ınd the girl. He pictured the blown-apart body prawled in the dirt, he saw again the tears track down the brown, freckled face. Her soft words, the warmth to her eyes that brought a heat to him. Anything to block out the terror that came from the faceless white form lashed to the rock.

The scream came to form words that stopped the pain. "I'll tell you, I'll sign anything. It was Adderson shot Maldinado, Adderson put that rope over you. It was Adderson."

Mickey turned his knife twice in the clean sand and returned it to its sheath. He looked at the sagging white man. Stripes of blood ran slowly down his blue-veined leg, pooled at the fleshy pocket above the knee, then fell in tired drops to the ground. The man had lasted longer than Mickey had thought. Not long enough for Mickey's taste.

His brothers came to stand next to him. They spoke softly, and Mickey answered, keeping one eye on the tall and dark-haired man who had not yet moved. Then Ketah picked up the small bundle of his belongings and pulled out the yellow striped blouse that spoke of his rank. Joseph shrugged into his own version of the blouse, which lacked the constriction of sleeves.

They walked past the tall, young white man, brushing shoulders against him, taking his nod as their due. They mounted two horses, rode around the piling of rock that blocked off the small gully, and were gone.

It was Mickey who untied the ropes and released Vace Yarborough, but would not give the man his clothes. He did allow him a scant cup of the bitter offee, then propelled the shivering man to stand where Blue was settled.

He did not look up, but handed Vace three sheets of paper and a thick stub of shaved pencil.

"You write it all down. Every word. And I'll see Mickey keeps to the other side of the fire. All of it, Vace. Every goddamn word."

It was hard for him to keep the anger from surfacing, hard to keep his hands off the puke-white face. What Mickey and his kin had done only captured Blue's anger and magnified it. He was shaken to find he had grown accustomed to the sounds and the screaming, and had relished the pain Yarborough was feeling. It would never be enough to wipe out the pain he had caused.

Blue clamped down on his temper and shortened his words. He stood slowly, finally wanting to face his enemy. Vace Yarborough did not take the paper. His hands hung from limp arms, his body shook with the early chill, yet he was too broken to hug himself and shiver into warmth. Blue rolled up the paper and jabbed at the hairless chest. Vace's head came up to stare at Blue, then look aside. The hands were slower, but they finally took the paper and let it unroll in loose fingers.

Vace sat down hard and stared at the whiteness in his hands. He had no idea how to start and what must be said. Blue watched the continuing silence, then spoke.

"You put down how you ambushed me with Adderson. Why you was after me. I heard you talking about the mare and using her to warn Señor Maldinado. You put that down in writing." He waited and watched the laborious writing appear on the page.

"It was you killed the weanlings. Write that out, tell them why. Then go to work on leaving Adderson to kill the Señor. Get it all down. Even how you framed me in town, setting those folks on us and killing Annuncio. Bet you fired that shot. I want all of it Vace."

It took a long time, but Yarborough wrote out each word, pausing to work over his thoughts, writing for his life. Blue looked once at Mickey and caught the downpull of his smile. It was a bitter victory, and unfinished. But they watched Vace write his confession, and there was a release of new hope in them both.

They wouldn't let him sleep. Blue tossed Vace his shirt and pants, and watched as the man dressed, saw him wince as he drew on the smelly long johns over his pinpricked leg and punctured groin. Mickey quickly broke camp as if he knew where they were going. Blue accepted his lead and worked alongside the reticent Indian.

"Ketah spoke to me of a small group of soldiers and where they are camped. We go to them, to their chief and have him listen. They will sign this paper with honor. Ketah say we can trust these soldiers."

This was the next step in the slow return to justice. Blue nodded his relief. He even helped the limping Yarborough mount the chestnut gelding. He would de behind the man, keep a gun loose in his hand. fter getting the bit of paper witnessed, Blue had iought of how he would get it to the town law. Riding ito the city of Tucson would open him to a bullet. Iickey would be scalped and hung before he got past ie streambed. And Yarborough would be with friends.

This time the trail took them down the eastern side f the mountains into the river basin. Mickey let them op to water the horses and splash the coolness of the ver over their dirt-streaked faces. Blue took handfuls f bottom sand and scrubbed at his hair, dunking his ead under the flowing water to remove the stain. He 'atched the lines of black dye weave into the current nd disappear. He worked his head over twice, feeling ie tingle that the sand left, then burrowed under the 'ater again, coming up with a mouthful that he spat ito the clear air. One shake of his head and the newly lond strands slapped into his eyes. He looked through iem to see Mickey watching, arms on knees, butt esting on his heels. There was a bright grin on the ark face that Blue knew was mirrored by his own nile.

Yarborough thought he saw a chance and reached for ie chestnut's bit. Two hands gripped him, digging eep into his shoulder muscle at the neck. The voice 'as Blue's; the grip belonged to the Indian.

"Not this time, Vace. You come along with us. Iount up.

It was a pleasure to walk the horses along the river-ank. The bottom land was flat and rich, growing miles of pale green spring grass. To their right ros steep-etched cliffs; beyond the reach of the water, t the east, the land went back to its scrub hills of cactu and spiky grass. They followed the river's course an took their delight from the moist land, the greenness c the cottonwoods, the signs of small game.

After an easy hour, Mickey picked up the pace, alte nating from a trot to a quick bursting run, then breather and a few minutes of walk. The land change with subtle signs like thinning grass and sma clumped plants. The horses strained to take the sma hills at a trot; the riders braced themselves to com down into the washes. To their right, the mountain slowed their height, dipping down to become soft hills.

Blue wiped the pooled sweat from his neck, pulle his hat off and ran the bandanna across his forehea They were moving south fast now. He watche Yarborough closely. There were several times whe the man rode too loose in the saddle, almost tipping o from the ragged-gaited horse. Mickey never looke back. He would pull to a stop and cock his head, wai then push his brown back into the long swing of th trot.

Mickey stopped and signaled Blue to come u beside him. As he pushed the dun past Yarborough Blue tried to look into the man's face. Head down, fac averted, the blue eyes refused contact, and Vac sagged into the swell of the saddle. Blue pulled th rein from his hand and dallied it around the narro orn of this old hull. He had no trust in the man, beaten r not.

Mickey did not turn his head and Blue settled the un beside him.

“There is a camp ahead. They are soldiers, three of iem, and one chief. They do nothing but wait. I stay ere, with him. You go.”

It was a short walk to the camp. Blue kept to lickey’s direction and watched for a sign. The camp vas not hidden. It was laid out in the center of an lmost level bowl, hills swelling around it. It was not war camp, not with the fire circle started and bedrolls tacked neatly against mesquite bush.

Three horses stood quietly at the picket line, tails oing against the afternoon pests. Blue halted the dun s a man approached him. Hands folded in full sight cross the horn, he watched the rifle muzzle. It rose ently and found its center on Blue’s shirt, and was teadied by capable hands. Blue did not move. The un cocked one hind foot and settled sideways.

The voice, when it came, was behind him. Blue set is teeth and clamped down on the impulse to spin and ight. This was not a war mission.

“What are you wanting with us, son? And why did ou leave the other man behind with an Indian guard? omething we can do for you?”

★ Chapter 15

Blue pushed the dun horse around with his knee. Th man with the rifle came with him, taking big steps t keep the barrel pointed at his target. The circle com pleted, Blue faced the speaker.

A man well into middle age, with some good heigl to him. A square face half-covered with a gra streaked bush of whiskers, eyes that looked right int Blue, and a strong body clad in a canvas jacket an pants. It was the hat that set Blue off, a flat circle c woven straw with a rounded top, shading the man face but adding nothing to his dignity.

Blue grinned. The speaker's face opened into a slov smile that matched Blue's for pleasure. Then the thir man, rifle still held easily, barrel ready to come up an fire square into Blue, came to stand behind the olde man's shoulder. This one was pure army, even i civilian dress: shoulders back, eyes straight ahead, fee wide apart in parade stance. The faded yellow strip down his pant leg was the only visual confirmation c his identity.

Blue finally broke the grinning silence. "Mister, got me a problem you can help solve. My name's Blu Mitchell. Men in back of me, the Indian's name i Mickey, the other is one Vace Yarborough, lately c Tucson. Mickey and me, we got a confession of th truth in certain matters from Mr. Yarborough, and nee a witness to his signing. Hoping you could oblige."

It was pretty weak, not much of a story for a man to ang his decision on. Blue had gone over and over it, orking at the words, but he could find nothing better ian the blunt truth. The paper itself, when this man ead it, told it all. A second look at the man let Blue now the truth was the only way.

"Why have you chosen to come to my camp? Surely ou know that the Fort is not more than a day's ride om here, and you would find official witnesses there, nd the law, ready to deal with you. Is that your reason or coming to me, the presence of the law?"

Blue nodded. "An Indian, name of Ketah, said to ome here to you, that you were the one that would sten and help." He stumbled on the next words.

"The law wants me. For murder. And I got the proof iat says no. Them two men, the Indian's been riding ith me, the other can do the proving wrong. I don't ant to be riding into a gathering of folks with an idian beside me and a posted reader offering money n my head. Ketah said you were the man to help."

The last words were stuttered in a plea. Blue found imself battling to keep his gaze level, his eyes traight on the man with the questions. The nightmare ounded lame out here on the edge of the desert, in the rightness of daylight, with only one man asking ques-ons, and another holding a rifle. He did not really now why he had come here, or what was special bout this one man. Mickey had brought him here, and was for him to play out the hand.

Blue sat straighter in the saddle, right hand going for

the pistol on his hip. The rifle came up with him t steady its center as the guard leaned over to whisper question to his commander. Blue felt the isolation c sitting high on the dun horse, a frightening vulnera bility. He was wide open and exposed, at the mercy c the square-faced man and his aide. His belly rolle over, sending a sour taste flooding his mouth. The du picked up his off hind foot to stand square and ready

"Ketah is one of my scouts. Bring in your men an we will listen to the story."

The man turned away, exposing his wide back t Blue's handgun and temper. The guard stayed read watching Blue's hand, then let the rifle barrel dro away as the tall rider spun the dun horse and lope back to the two men waiting in the fold of the hill.

Mickey rode down to meet Blue, pulling the chestnu along, and paying no attention to the unwilling ride Blue swung in beside the Indian, and the three returne to the comfort of the small camp. The fire was stirre to life, and the soldier was cooking something in th black iron pan. Coffee boiled on the coals.

This time the voice came from behind the shoulde of a dark red mule. "Light down, tie up here. Enoug room on the line. We've got a bit of extra ration fc your mounts. Looks to me they need it."

Blue settled gingerly into the shallow depression o his heels. Mickey squatted down just back of hin knife still in its sheath, shoulders relaxed, hand swinging free from his knees. Vace Yarborough wa ear them, tied with rawhide thongs to the thickest of e mesquite bushes. The straw-hatted man had the aper, and did not lift his head from the reading of it hen the soldier wordlessly passed out cups of coffee. lue welcomed having something to do with his ands, to take away the edginess of sitting still. He rank the coffee he did not want, and felt the bitter quid stir in his belly.

Mickey must have felt the agitation, for the Indian ut a hand to Blue's shoulder and pressed quickly, then ised his cup in a salute to the straw-hatted man who as still reading. Blue copied the gesture and forced imself to relax. They were at the mercy of this man, ut Ketah said he was the one, and Mickey knew ough to believe his brother.

"This reads very clearly, Mr. Mitchell. But one ques-on. How did you get this man out of Tucson? I don't eed to ask the reason for the man's willingness to lk, but I would like to know about his abduction."

His eyes flickered from the impassive dark face of e Indian to settle on the odd ocean-green eyes of the oung man. The paper he held in his fingers, with its wkward spellings and labored words, gave only part f the story. He was intrigued.

The story sounded unreal as Blue told of the long fternoon and evening he spent in Tucson, waiting r his opportunity to take Yarborough away from his afety and his companions. It was hard to match the lder man's stare as he talked, and the words were ometimes slow in coming. But when he finished, the man slapped his knee in wonder, and laughed.

"It seems to me, Mr. Mitchell, that some of the tim you have acted with less than good sense, but you hav never lacked for guts, my friend. What do you plan t do with this Mr. Yarborough once I sign your docu ment? You cannot just turn him loose, and the law wi most likely grab you first if you enter the city with hi in tow with only your word."

Blue shook his head. This man was way ahead c him everywhere he turned. "Been going one step at time, sir." He found the title slipped out easily. Micke grunted what sounded like agreement. "If I up and ki him, the law won't be satisfied, and I'll either hang c run. Can't turn him loose, and can't bring him to tow on my own. Best to leave him with Mickey and sort out with the law, then come back for him."

For the first time Vace Yarborough brought up h head and protested. He sat up against the pull of th rope around his neck and waved his bound hands.

"You can't leave me with that damned savage. He' kill me first chance. Him and those two others. Be ou right vicious to leave me with him." The absurdity c his words sank in, and Yarborough knew his defe: was complete. He sank back to his reclining positio face flushed, sweat beading across his forehead. H eyes shifted between the two men, never quite meetin their gaze.

The square-faced man spoke first; "There is a sin pler and more humane solution. I can send him back t the fort under guard, which will free you to ride bac ıd sort out your own skirmish with the law. Mickey ay stay with us where he will be safe. You will only ıve your own safety to be of concern."

Blue did not have time to nod his acceptance. The ·ay whiskered man continued as if it were all anned. "My time is short. In a few days I will be aving Arizona. Yesterday I watched the trains take vay some of my enemies, and some of my friends. ut there is time for me yet, and I can do this one more ing. All right, Mr. Mitchell, give me your prisoner ıd I will escort him back to the fort. But first, stay ıd eat dinner with us. There will be rabbit and beans ady in a few moments."

Two men had come to the camp, one carrying two 'inchesters, one holding a brace of rabbit. They nored the conference and went about their chores, ıd soon a good smell had grown from the cooking e. Blue glanced at Mickey, ready to take his next ove from him, but there was no need. The Indian was otionless on his heels; his hand moved in a vague rcle of greeting. Mickey grinned at the worry he saw the odd eyes. At times this one was too old.

"I need a pen, Wilson. And introduce these gen- men to O'Donnell and Niebling. They will be ining us for dinner. Gentlemen." He sat on the con- nience of a rock, and the document was signed with flourish and handed back to Blue.

The relief that flooded him made the words sound ick and stupid. He stammered a thank you and orked at saying more.

"It is not over for you yet, my friend. You still ha your ride into the city, and your confrontation with t law, as well as your search for the man nam Adderson. It is not yet over. But please, do rest up a join us for dinner before you ride."

Blue walked past Mickey to the picketed horses. stood by the dun and leaned his weight into the safe of the solid horse. Eyes closed, he rested in t familiar warmth of the animal's smell. Then he fou his balance again, and opened his eyes. The docume felt brittle in his hands, the words holding his life. started rolling the paper, anxious to pack it safely a ride out. The bold signature across the bottom of t page read "George C. Crook."

★ Chapter 16

Tucson was getting itself civilized; even had a Ch of Police and deputies, no more dependence on a to marshal and a few rowdy gunslingers to keep t peace. One of these deputies, making his late-nig rounds, walked into the flat out body of Bris Adderson. Damning the drunks who thought th could sleep where they fell, he rolled the snoring m back into the side alley, cursing all the time his gre bulk. The early morning darkness hid the swelli bruise that covered the side of his head.

There was a time, as he woke up, when Bristol cou remember nothing—name, place, even the year. W the hell was he and what in God's name was he doi leeping in a pile of horse shit? He gagged at the weetness of the crumbly texture filling his mouth, and olled over to land in a fresher pile. Anger beat aside ne pain in his head.

Then the curses started, and the familiar roll of the ords juggled in his mind, bringing up a name, an xtra face. Then the events of the night flooded him. 'ace was gone. Some goddamned greaser got a hold f his horse and he was gone. Vace would 'a come ack if he got free. Bristol grabbed on to that fact, and uilt his memories around it. Vace would come back or him.

He patted down his vest pockets, then stood to lean is bulk on the coolness of the livery wall. Hands went ver his pants, seeking anything that would buy him nother drink. He ran his tongue around in his mouth, igging at the mush imbedded in his teeth. Spitting dry id nothing; he had to have whiskey to get cleaned out.

God damn it. The cursing started again. Not a dime n him, not even a useless bastard penny. And no sign f Vace.

Bristol made it to the dim inside of the stable in a eries of staggering steps. The face and the voice that reeted him were not what he wanted, and the cursing valed his own efforts. Bristol stood flatfooted for the ecture that finally ended with something he could nderstand. He didn't like it, but it was something to ang on to for now.

". . . And you and that son-of-a-bitching partner of ours, thinking you can ride out 'a here day and night, then come stumbling back in the morning looking lik a strangled hound and wanting help. Well, I tell yo mister, I been talking to the police. They tell me wha I can do with deadbeats likes 'a you. You owe me tw day's rent on them broncs. That's four goddamn dol lars 'merican. And you gonna work off that money a a dollar a day, can sleep in the loft or wherever yo damned well find a bed. But you come here and work damn you, till your pard comes back with ther broncs. Or I get them policemen to set you up pretty i jail."

There was more, mostly about his lineage and hi parents' doubtful marriage, and Bristol let it go righ over him. Wasn't nothing he ain't heard before. H knew there was a place for him, where he could wa and watch for Vace. The pinch-faced man's tempe finally ran down, settled by the string of words. H even had enough pity in him to hand the smelly drun a lukewarm cup of coffee before he put him to work Horses don't wait for a man's head to clear before the dump on the barn floor. He handed over the three-tine fork and motioned to Bristol. Shovel from here t here, and get at it.

He knew now it had been a mistake to sit at the fir and take dinner with the General. Yet Micke motioned for him to stay, to eat, and had accepted hi own plate of the rabbit stew and beans, pushing asid the strangeness of the spoon to use his knife. Eve Vace Yarborough had been untied and set down to ea

Րhe neck rope stayed in place, insuring his finishing he meal with them.

Blue had been fascinated as he watched the whey-colored face catch the quick flash of Mickey's knife. Րhe Indian shoveled in the beans and thick bits of tew. Vace Yarborough had to be thinking back to the lawn, and the painful tracks that same knife had made ıp into the privacy of his groin. He saw Yarborough :lamp down on his lower lip and turn away, hand in nidair, shaking the piece of rabbit free from the spoon.

Now Blue knew the same shaking. He rubbed his ıand deep into his eyes. He had to stay awake, keep ıis mind alert. He could not count back to when he had lept. The hour of dozing before dawn had been his irst time down in more than two days.

The dun took advantage of his rider's slowing esponses, and stopped to tear into a palo verde, then vandered to a more tempting clump of grass. Blue let he horse stand and graze. There was something more mportant that had to be reasoned with and figured out. Damned if he could remember what.

Timing. The flat expanse of desert waved in heat as ar as he could see. The soldiers behind him said the ide to Tucson was a long eight hours on a fresh horse. That made no sense. It would put him into the city past nidnight, right into the heart of the late-night drunken ights, with no guarantee he would find the law before t, or someone else, found him. It was so easy Blue started to laugh, spooked the dun, and found himself ying in a cactus looking up at the underjaw of the star-

tled horse. He'd seen a picture of a camel once, some
thing the army been playing around with; damned i
the dun gelding didn't look like one of them cusse
beasts from down here.

The laughter took over. Blue's shoulders rocked, hi
whole body gave in to the laughter that started t
choke him. He grabbed the curious dun and found hi
balance to stand up.

Sleep. That was the answer to his timing problem
Life-giving, time-wasting sleep. A few hours nov
would put him in Tucson early morning. So obvious i
had to jump up and grab him out of the saddle befor
he figured it out.

A twist in the dry wash, a tumble of rock near a
overhang of exposed mesquite roots. No graze, but th
dun had finished a nose bag at the campsite. Blue tie
the reins to his boot, wadded his vest under his head
tilted his hat, and lay back. After a few minutes, th
dun tugged at the restraint of the reins, cocked his hea
at the strange sounds coming from the long body, an
lowered his head to rest.

There was only one horse. The brown gelding
walking in very slowly, keeping one foreleg off th
ground in a hobbling, three-legged jump. Only on
horse, led by a dark-skinned figure, black hair braide
and wrapped in bright cloth. Only one horse, only on
man.

She ran. Picked up the hem of her long skirt and sh
ran, straight for the Indian, feet hitting the hardpacke

ground and leaving a trail of settling dust. The early sun blinded her; perhaps there was another horse, another rider yet out of sight.

"Mickey, where is he? Is he all right? What happened? Please. Don't tell me he's been hurt. Mickey."

The brown horse was sweated and dripping, his glossy coat turned a dull tan with the salt. Too tired and too sore to even pick up his ears at the flapping great skirt or the flailing arms, the brown gelding welcomed the chance to stand, and lowered his head until his muzzle almost touched dirt.

"He take piece of paper to Tucson to find law. He need help. You ride."

The trembling weakened the horse: legs shaking, side rippling in pain, neck bowed, knees beginning to buckle. Mickey felt the horse start to go down, and lashed at the animal with the reins, jerking hard on the bit, savaging the tender mouth to keep the horse from giving up.

"Miss, take stick and hit hard, keep horse moving. We get him to the ranch. I treat him. Hit harder."

It took five more long and impatient minutes for the hobbling brown to find the comfort of a soft-bedded shed. Five more minutes of Mickey's labored story. Celita did not wait to see her father's once-favored horse go down on its side in the sweetness of the cured winter grass. Mickey would heal the animal, or tend it until its death. It was now for her to get to Tucson.

"Mama, Mama." Her voice echoed in the morning darkness of the house. Celita skidded to a stop and listened. There was a series of soft noises in the smal room from the kitchen, where Blue had lain for s long, where others had passed their burial night. It wa here her mother had chosen to grieve alone.

"Mama, Blue's riding into Tucson. Mickey says he' got a paper proving he didn't kill Papa. I've got to hel him."

There was a smile waiting for her as she came int the small room. A tentative smile, drawn from the line of sadness.

"Yes, Celita. You must go to him, but go with calmness, not in panic. There will be trouble enough Now tell me what Mickey has told you. And I will hel you get ready. You must take him what he will hav need of."

Her mother did nothing more than nod at the shor tale retold by her daughter. She moved slowly throug the house, listening while they pulled out a pair o pants, a tough canvas jacket, a faded shirt. It took nail and a hammer to punch another two holes in th belt that would carry the holster around Celita's waist

Mickey had a horse roped out and waiting, a toug blue roan standing barely fourteen hands, chosen t run the distance to the old mud walls of the tow without effort. It was Ruth Maldinado who brough out the cartridge belt and the Winchester. He daughter's small saddle gun would not do.

The fast-moving excitement kept Celita fron thinking. She reacted to everything: the quickness o her mother's hands, the harsh nicker from the roa pony, the smell and feel of the unfamiliar weight of the gun and holster at her hip. It was when she slowed down to tie the smooth leather straps around the saddle bags that she knew what she was doing. And why.

Blue Mitchell. The feel of those long hands, the safety found in leaning against his chest, the look to those startling blue-green eyes. It was for him. Celita's hands stopped in midair, still holding onto the half-tied knot. She was afraid.

Her mother saw the fear, and wrapped a strong arm around her daughter.

"You are going for him, and he will be there for you when this is over. Go with him, child. Fight for him, and when it is over, tell him you love him. And go with my blessing . . . and that of your father."

There was no time for the tears. Celita hugged the sturdy body, holding on a long time, yet becoming impatient to ride. She slipped onto the roan's back and swung the little horse around in a high circle over his hocks. The blue horse bolted from the ranch, freed to run his heart out by the lightweight rider on his back.

Ruth Maldinado did not watch her daughter leave. She went to the small shed and the downed horse, to stand with the silent Indian and watch the labored breathing of the once-fine animal. She turned her mind away from the wild ride and the angry law in Tucson. There was nothing more she could do.

Clement Proctor was proud of his job, and scared of it. Chief of Police. A good title for a man to lay claim of.

Had it less than a year and was still getting used to it Hard to keep up with Buttner's reputation as a tough man. But Clement G. Proctor was getting a handle on the routine and making some of his own mark on the lawless in the city.

Routine was the answer. Like now, him sitting here at his desk before the rest of the town was moving going over last night's reports, making his plans fo the day. Not just letting things happen, but directing them. Hell, he even went over the new readers each morning, with his coffee, checking for faces he migh need to know. Went over the old ones, too, reac quainting himself with those wanted by the law.

A lot of the bad ones drifted through Tucson, going on its reputation as a town easy on the lawless. Fig uring it for a wide open town. No longer, not while Clement Proctor was the Chief of Police here.

He really liked that title.

The town was starting to move, mostly wagons still coming in for supplies or moving goods through town The barber shop would be opening in ten minutes Proctor looked forward to getting a clean shave every day. He rubbed a smooth hand across the stubble. A good barbering could be the making of a man's day He liked to think it was a symbol of the continuing civ ilization of Tucson.

Proctor's head turned. He could count the footsteps Be at the door in four more beats. John Calder Hollen beck; his deputy. Good man with a gun, short, pow erful, John ran the office while the chief was getting his shave and testing the temper of the city. A good man, Hollenbeck, short on size and humor, but, by God, accurate with his gun.

Proctor stood up and pushed back the sturdy oak chair. One arm in his black frock coat, he nodded to the deputy and stepped around him to the street. He finished shrugging into the coat while he stood outside. Not good for the Chief to be seen walking the street in a mended vest and rolled up sleeves. He took a deep breath. It was going to be another good day.

★ Chapter 17

He liked a town this time of day. The streets were silent, the air clear of dust. A man could ride easy without bumping into seven more. In the three blocks he'd ridden so far, there had been only one person out walking. The bowed head had come up with unfocused morning eyes, and the half-turned flip of the hand became a salute between rider and citizen.

The tiredness was gone from Blue. Even the dun had an eagerness to his step that gave lie to the past eight hours of travel. Not hard running, but a steady trot that took in the miles. Even so, eight hours covered a lot of distance.

The closest he got to thinking things to a logical end was to hunt out the law real early, at gunpoint if necessary. Then force the law to read the paper and acknowledge it. Then he would get to Adderson. The man would probably stay in town without Vace, if he was up and moving from the merciful kick of the buckskin horse.

Blue crossed the main street, and knew the name of the street from the sign painted bright and clear and hanging from a gaslight post. There were more people now, hurrying to get somewhere fast. Blue found breathing difficult; any one of these good folk could look up at him and remember the description. He dropped his eyes, stopped looking around. Better off asking questions than running the risk of a whole mob seeing him.

There was one man not in a hurry. Wearing a clean black coat, looked formal, almost like an undertaker. A tall, clean-shaven man, clean everywhere. Bright white shirt, soft tan pants, and polished boots. A real good citizen. Only the pistol hung low at his hip gave Blue pause, but the man looked right at him and grinned his "good morning." Blue asked his directions and got sent down the street and to the right. Nice and polite. Blue tipped his hat in thank you.

There was a dark bay tied to the railing. A real solid horse, clean lines, good rigging, and a fancy new Winchester stuck in the scabbard. Guess the owner felt tying up in front of the law would protect his property. Blue tied the dun at the opposite end of the railing, and slapped the horse when a hoof came up to threaten his new neighbor.

Here it was. The office of the law. Only in this town it was called the Police Station. Still a jail, still the end to a man's freedom, and his life, if he guessed wrong.

Blue hacked twice to clear his throat, and his right hand patted the precious folded piece of paper in the buttoned safety of his vest.

The man seated at the scarred desk looked the part. Wide shoulders, a heavy moustache covering his face, shirt frayed at the collar, with the badge of his profession pinned at an angle on his left pocket. He barely looked up, but did offer a grunt when Blue walked into the small office. Blue stayed on the near side of the close room; this was as far as he could force himself.

The smell was the same. Being in the Arizona territory didn't make this jail any different from the others Blue'd been in. He coughed again, looked to spit, then swallowed. The man behind the desk still did not look up.

Until Blue's hand went to his pocket and fumbled for the paper. Then the brown-capped head came up, and a hand grasped a small shiny revolver on the desk, hammer pulled back, barrel pointed at Blue. He read the sign; better get the explanation started before the law blew his head off. His sweat slicked the edges of the paper together and left Blue trying to pick them apart. He started talking.

"Says here, I'm Blue Mitchell, got a confession about the killing of Rafael Maldinado . . ."

There was no more time. The blocky man pushed back the chair and swung out beyond the desk, hand bringing up the short muzzle of the gun, aiming it directly at Blue.

"Got your nerve, mister. Give you that. Put up your hands and shuck that paper. You're wanted for murder.

That's nothing a bit of paper'll change. Got the reader right here."

This wasn't right. Blue had made no threat to the man, had come on peaceful, gun holstered, rifle out on the dun. He held out the paper and tried again.

"This paper here proves . . ."

He took one step toward the man, waving the separated sheets that held the rest of his life.

"Mister, you put that damned paper down and step back, hands raised like I told you. Maybe then I'll look at your paper."

The pages fluttered to the desk top. Instead of reaching for them, the man dug into a desk drawer and brought out handcuffs. He tossed them across the desk to Blue.

"Put them on and turn around."

Blue looked at the bit of paper, lost on the official mess of reward dodgers, descriptions, and complaints littering the shiny oak. Hands bound in the metal cuffs, he would have no way of forcing the law to look at the paper, no way to defend himself. He hadn't come to Tucson to give up, but to fight. He bent down to pick up the cold metal, struggled with them and then looked at the law in confusion and held out the cuffs.

With a quick twist he threw them hard at the square face. At the same time he dove for the desk, frantic to get his hands on the paper. The deputy reached for the handcuffs out of instinct, the same instinct that made him pull the trigger.

The blast almost by the side of his head, deafened

Blue. There was a momentary burn down his arm as he skidded across the desk, nose buried in paper. The deputy brought the small pistol up again, almost directly in front of Blue's face. He stepped back and slid on the metal cuffs. The gun fired again; the bullet tore into the adobe wall behind Blue.

Blue shoved from his boot toes and skated across the desktop, sending papers flying, and propelled himself into the solid man. They landed flat on the plank floor. The law's head hit the wood with a hollow thump, and Blue felt the body underneath him go limp. It was over before it got started. He sat back, knees on either side of the solid body, and swiped at the water collecting under his hat.

There were footsteps running outside, headed towards the small office. Many footsteps, voices yelling, men keyed up by the shooting. Blue was frantic. He dug through the mass of paper, desperate to find the two sheets. It was strange; as he rooted in the shifting piles, he saw bright red stains, some fresh enough to puddle before soaking into the paper fibers. He looked down at his arm where it burned, and wondered at the length of red showing through the dull blue of the sleeve. It confused him. He craned his head to look at the inside of his elbow. A dark gray circle was centered by a welling of blood. He'd been hit by the first shot.

There was no pain, and his fingers flexed when he tried them. Blue dropped to his knees to get at what he hoped were his papers, and found the description of himself on the faded reader. No wonder the law was quick to shoot.

There it was, buried under last night's report. Blue rolled the two pieces together and stuffed them in his back pants pocket. He leaned over to pick up the loose gun. A quick check showed it was empty, and he threw it in the corner as hard as he could. It bounced and slid under a chair.

He was still waiting. He had heard the sounds of men running, recognized the wild yells that came right after the two shots. Then Blue put his head back and laughed. Tucson wasn't as civilized as the good folks would have it. The yelling was across the street, men gathering in a tight group to slap each other on the back. Either news of a gold strike or more about the Indians. The two shots from the office of the law had gone unnoticed.

It was simple to walk out the front door, close it gently, and turn right to walk away from the sleeping dun and the powerful-looking bay. The small group across the street had split up, some standing in twos and threes to talk eagerly. No one bothered with one more seedy-looking drifter. They were interested in their own news.

He stayed close to the buildings. If anyone was to pass him on the right, they could not help but see the red streaks down his arm. Pain began, slight at first then bursting into a full bouquet. God almighty, it hurt Let him know with each step he had to do something and soon.

A warmth ran down into his palm, dripped off the ends of his fingers to spot the ground. Blue put his left hand at the top of his upper arm near his shoulder and found the crease, slick with blood. Sweat covered his forehead as he drew his fingertips down the arm, following the diagonal curve of the crease as it crossed his biceps to the inside of his elbow. The furrow was deeper there, and the fabric of the shirt was burned black. The law had been aiming at the top of his head as he dove across the desk. Blue shuddered.

It made no sense. He couldn't wander around Tucson looking like a victim of the Indian wars and waiting for a lawman to wake up and cry murder. He turned another corner, hesitated as the progression of storefronts seemed familiar. Halfway down the street, on the other side, was the dubious safety of Mr. Warner's Mercantile.

Wagons crossed in front of Blue. A man slammed into him and mumbled something that could be his manners or a curse. There was a ringing in Blue's ears, a distance between him and his legs. He couldn't stand here, yet there was a reason he could not walk across the street and into the calmness of the store. Another man bumped into him, jolted him hard, and Blue remembered, as the pain of his arm echoed behind his eyes. Blood. But he had to move on.

Soon someone would walk into the shambles of the law office and wake the stunned man. If Blue stood here like a poleaxed steer much longer, he might as well burn the papers and hang himself. Save the city the trouble.

A heavy ranch wagon started the turn down the street. Blue gauged his steps, and came off the walkway to fit in behind the wagon, then moved to the other side, walking close to the big, slow turning wheel. The driver didn't look back, but watched a too-well-dressed lady make her way so very carefully along the edge of the street.

Blue stayed with the wagon until it crossed paths with a high-stepping team of blacks. He followed their wake, angling closer to the invitation of the open door. One foot on the walk and he met eyes with a kid who looked back at him, then at his arm, and almost got his mouth open to scream. Blue growled at the child, a boy of no more than five. Growled fiercely to match the pain in his arm, and the panic driving him. The boy turned and fled into the skirts of his mother, who reached down absently and patted his head.

He walked into the store as if there were no blood on him, no law after him, no crowd wanting him. Stepped into the blessing of the dark walls shelved floor to ceiling, half-empty now but holding a promise. He took the path he remembered, the path the frantic bay gelding had slid along. Past the steep railings of the stairway, careful to duck his head at the right-angled supports, then through the unlocked door into the storeroom.

Not until he closed the door behind him and stood for a moment did he hear the voices. The clatter of his heeled boots had blocked out the sound. A sweet sound like Celita's voice. Blue shook his head, noted with lisinterest the droplets of blood that flipped from the nds of his fingers and stained the white bags of new lour.

Celita. She looked up in the middle of her talking vith Mr. Warner and saw him. Swaying back and forth n the uneven wearing of his boots, barely able to tand. The dust-thickened light blotted his outlines, ut she could see him. It took only a quick word to Mr. Varner and she came to him, walking with a measured race, head high, eyes carrying a private welcome. She valked to him like a woman grown, with a dignity eyond her years.

Only three steps from Blue—close enough to see the leasure in his face, the tightness at his mouth, the pain rawing his eyes—she became a child again. Her arms ame up as she skittered forward, and her head landed ust right, under his collarbone. Her arms went around im and Blue did not feel their tightness against the urned muscle of his wound.

He lost track of the time. Then Charlie Warner stood t his shoulder, white rolls of cloth and an untopped vide-mouth jar stacked in the crook of his arm. His ther hand was holding the back of a slatted chair. Varner put the chair down hard; the echo of the small egs hitting the dusty floor brought Celita's eyes back nto focus.

Blue untangled the girl and turned to sit down, lost is balance in the spinning of his head, and felt the ardness of the caned seat slap his butt as he sat down. Ie shook his head at the distress in Celita's face.

"There's no time, girl. I left one of the police lyin flat on his back in the office. Got to find one of the la around here willing to read a paper. Mighty importar to me."

"Mickey told me about the paper. I'll help, Blue. S will Mr. Warner."

Blue jerked his arm away from the gentle hands an tried to stand. Celita put a hand to his chest an pushed.

"You set and let me talk. We've got it figured. M Warner says that Clement Proctor is the chief, he's th one who might listen. He's the one we've got to find. Her face contorted into a frown. "Describe the ma you fought, the one in the office. It can't be M Proctor."

"Short, beefy, brown hair and whiskers. Wouldn listen to whatever I said."

Warner interrupted. "Good, that's Hollenbeck Proctor's a tall fellow, slicked-back hair and clea face. Usually over to the barber's this time of th morning."

He turned to the girl and handed her the wide mouthed jar.

"You finish up here. The arm isn't bad, just mess Your mother taught you well enough. I'm going to th barbershop. Mitchell, you give me the paper and b here when I get back. This will be the safest place i town for you. Time Hollenbeck comes to, the whol town'll be buzzing with your name and planning o spending the reward. Liable to potshot you jus valking back to the police station. You set right here."

God, Warner talked a lot when he got going. Blue ingered the folded square of paper, then looked into Varner's face and handed the man the priceless bit of aper. Then Warner was gone, hat placed squarely on is thinning hair.

Celita put two fingers to his lips and shushed him ;ently, not letting Blue get his feet under him. Leave it o Mr. Warner, she said. And then she took the long-andled scissors and picked at the top of the torn leeve, dragging it away from his shoulder. Blue felt he coolness of the air ruffle the fine hair on his arm as he blades stroked clean. The only sign of her distress vas the almost silent intake of breath as Celita peeled he material away, starting at the top, lifting each hread of the stained cotton as it stuck to his flesh.

Blue tried to match her breath for breath, holding his s she worked the unraveled bit of cloth from the xposed white edge of his muscle, easing out the tension to get ready for the next tug. He wanted desperately to reach forward and touch his mouth to the fine weat at her hair line, to somehow take from her the ain she was holding. His arm was numb, as if she had bsorbed the fire.

Then she caught her lower lip in her teeth and varned him with her averted eyes. The smell gagged im before the flash burned down into his belly, earing at him in a wheeling of pain. He refused the ffer of a deadening drink, just shook his head and urned his face away. He was not capable of words. If he opened his mouth now, it would be to scream. Th whiskey burned its path down his arm, and washed clean, cold path to his fingers. Then the fire died to a icy burn.

The smell of the salve was familiar to him, and wel come. Pine tar, turpentine, linseed oil. A good concoc tion to heal any open sore on a horse, to keep awa flies and infection. Celita used the salve's oily thick ness to fill in the tunnel dug by the bullet, gently pat ting the evil smell level with the untouched flesh of hi arm. The bandage wound around the upper arm put strength back in his arm, as if he could feel the repai and lean into the support.

Celita leaned down and kissed him. Quickly, on th mouth. Then stood back to admire her work.

"Miss, I got to get to Adderson. Been thinking ove Mr. Warner's words. If Bristol hears I hit town, he'l run. And I owe him too much to let him go now. He' the one fired on your pa. Get me a gun, I'm going afte him."

He saw the look in her eye. He knew it, from the firs day he rode the bay gelding against her wishes. Blu stood and took one step toward the girl; she backed u one step. He tried one more step, and she moved awa from him again.

"Miss. I thank you again. You're kind to help, to b here. But I got to . . ."

"And you haven't learned a thing. Adderson's bully. He'll beat you to a pulp or . . . Damn it, he' more than you can take."

They were both shocked by her words. Blue liked er caring. No one ever cried for him before.

"Me and Bristol, we go back a long way. I got a sign n him and he knows it. All I need to do is find him nd he'll run right into my fist. He's too close now to et go."

Blue shrugged his right arm, smiled at the numbed hrobbing. "You did a good job here, don't feel a thing. his won't slow me down none."

It was a lie; the slight movement woke a warning pasm through his shoulder and back. Blue widened is smile, remembering how it felt to grin at his ene-nies and watch the anger draw past their common ense.

Then the insolence came back full term to match the ureness of his words. Damn it, he had a fixed arm, a etter turning him free, and an old grudge to settle with he fat-faced son who'd roped him and hog-tied him to e shot.

"He got your pa, miss. I can't let that go."

Blue looked down at his hands, spread the ten fin-ers wide, and flexed them, made two fists. He would ot admit to the line running up to his shoulder. The ands worked, and that was all he needed for now.

He could take Bristol Adderson.

★ Chapter 18

It felt good. Have to tell Rosa how good it felt. To b doing something again, not the kind of doing where h stood behind the counter and measured dusty fabric o shoveled out dried beans by the pound. The anger an the ever-present need for a drink were gone, replace by a lightness inside that pleased him.

Warner ran his fingers through the thick growth o brush at his jowls. Chief Proctor had a good idea keeping clean shaven, and doing it every day; put sense of duty and honor back in a man. Maybe afte this fracas was over, he'd take himself to the barbe get the vegetation trimmed to a respectable quarter inch. Warner's step quickened. Right now he neede to find the law, and fast.

He stayed on the opposite side of the police station almost skipping his steps in his hurry to turn the corne and see the wide painted stripes of the barber pole. Th growing cluster of men who'd been yahooing thei celebration earlier had shifted sides of the street, an more were ganging around the half-open door. Damn That meant Hollenbeck was discovered and the wor was out.

One man detached himself from the group, angled path across the busy street, and came to the walkwa almost at Charlie's back. Charlie acted on his impuls and stopped suddenly, forcing the man to walk into him He turned and spread his arms in abject apology an

eld onto the man, patting him as if to look for damage.
"Why, sir, I am most apologetic, how rude of me to ump you so. There is no excuse for my behavior."

For a moment Charlie Warner forgot his mission and njoyed his part, overwhelming the man with verbose indness. Confusion blanked the pale eyes of the hambling drifter as Charlie spun a profusion of words nd pats that would not allow the man to continue his urried errand.

"Is there anything I can do to show the depths of my eeling at this untimely interruption? Why I'm on my ay to the barbershop, but I can take more than a few inutes to repay you for the abject rudeness of my eatment of you." Careful there, Charlie, my boy, you re overdoing this.

The man's voice fit his condition; gravel rough and ard spoken. "I ain't cared nothing for your fussings, ister. Headed for the law down to Ansel's cutting hop. Got to get him out 'a there and back to his jail. ell, some outlaw come in and bashed the stuffings ut 'a his deputy. Got to find the law and get out oking. There's a reward out for this 'un, and I fancy get it."

"Why, my good man, I'm headed right now for nsel's barbershop. Be delighted to bring back your w for you and let you get started on your search for e desperado. Be most delighted to help."

Suspicion over the flow of words warred with greed. he chinless man snorted at Warner's offer, then spat nto the street.

"You tell Proctor that Hollenbeck's down, got lump the size of a horseapple back of his head. Wa that killer, Mitchell, done it. One that shot the mex while back. He'll know."

Right enough the chief of police would know Charles Warner would make certain the man knew everything. Charlie patted the folded papers buttone into his inside coat pocket. The lift came back to hi steps as he left the manhunter under the gentl swinging sign of the news vendors. LOCAL AND FOREIGN PAPERS FOR SALE. Tomorrow Charles Warner an company would be the news.

Ansel's wonderfully striped sign was easy to find Warner elbowed inside and found the chief almos asleep.

"Chief Proctor, my name is Charles Warner. I hav come on an errand of mercy. There is something I wis you to read that has a great deal of importance to yo and to a certain young couple. Please, there is no nee to interrupt your shave. . . . I can take the liberty c reading the document to you and then you may see for yourself. If you will allow . . ."

He stumbled some in his reading, awkward wit the half-mad spellings and smudged print. But th story came to the law with its treachery and gree clear and loud. Charlie Warner kept reading slowing the words as he came to the end, knowin that the law was waving aside the ministrations c the barber to come erect in the padded comfort c the chair, eyes wide, mouth pursed in a gentle, won ering whistle. The reading made for a good story.

Even Charlie took in a deep breath as he read the sig-ature of the witness. The kid hadn't said anything bout this. Charlie knew the importance of this partic-lar signature; there could be no doubting the veracity f the tale, not with this man as witness. His head jerked p from the dark scrolling of black ink that flourished cross the bottom of the second page. The Chief's tune-ess whistle became a loud exclamation of disbelief.

"Let me see that, mister. Damned if it reads true." But the willingness to believe was strong in the half-athered face. Charlie gave him the paper, gave him a ninute to run his eyes over the two wrinkled sheets, to tudy the lines of the well-known signature.

"The boy's in town right now, Chief. He's had a fight vith your deputy, Mr. Hollenbeck. Who, I gather, vould not listen to him and tried to put him in your ine jail.

"There is a mob out hunting for the boy right now, purred on by the meager offering of $50. They know e is in town, and will shoot to kill without mercy. What they don't know is that, right now, he is in my toreroom with the young woman whose father he is upposed to have killed. She has never believed the tory, and came to help him."

God, Charlie, say what you got to and let go. The oy's life is getting shorter and shorter and you're nterrupting his chances with your damned words. Charlie swore at himself; it was hard changing the abits of a long lifetime.

“Chief, come to my store. Then you and the boy ca walk back to your office, him in your custody. No on will fire on him. Then you can spread the word. Com with me now.”

Clement Proctor had reached the door before th shopkeeper had finished his story. The soap drying o his face itched, and the bristly hair cut from around hi ears dug sharp points into his neck. All that could wai Now he had to catch up with Mitchell and get him ou from the mob. Adderson and Yarborough being mixe up in this didn’t surprise him at all. And he wished t God that Warner for once would shut up.

The narrow alleys and close-set houses were his bes chance. But where to start looking? Blue eased hi back against the clay wall and pulled his hat dow over his eyes. Start where he’d seen Bristol last, th north end livery.

The clean shirt and borrowed frock coat gave hir some protection, some blurring of his identity. It wa hard just the same to walk the street in the ope without seeing an enemy in each doorway or slow ambling cowhand. There were some who slowe down as they came past him, eyeing Blue like a bron up for sale. The sweat dripped down his back, his righ arm throbbed, but Blue fumbled for something in hi coat pocket, kept his head turned, and walked an eas pace, fighting the hurry in his mind by drawing a slov grin on his face. He had to find Bristol Adderson.

The rounded shoulders, the sloping set to the thick

uscled back gave the man to him. Bent over a eaming pile of manure, Bristol Adderson was eaving his gut into the mound, getting rid of last ght's whiskey. Blue figured this made them even: ristol's belly and his arm. He didn't wait to add up e handicap and read them to the public.

Just one word. A shout. "Bristol."

The man's head came up, saliva stringing from his ack mouth. Adderson was a dumb brute but there as no hesitation in him. He roared into Blue, spittle ying, hands reaching to end the torment. Blue oliged the man. He ducked under the reaching arms nd rammed a doubled fist into the soft belly. Bristol ent with the force and stumbled, but came back faster an Blue figured.

A fist caught him in the arm, high up, almost at his houlder, spinning him into the barn door and bringing m to one knee. Adderson's follow-up blow hit the ood above Blue's head, splintering the board and rawing a howl from the man. Blue came up under his ms and drove a hard left to the ribs, then crossed ith a right under his chin.

That was a mistake. The damaged right arm muscle pasmed, turned numb, drew his fingers into a tight not. Adderson choked out an oath that fouled Blue's ce, then reached his spread hand to grip Blue's arm. lue fought against the hold and missed the right and aimed at his face, taking the blow across his heek. Adderson's left arm came back in a straight ne, elbow jamming into the split flesh of his face hard enough to send lights through Blue's eyes.

That released the numbness. Blue drew his left ba and short-armed Adderson in the gut. Once, twice, quick succession. The clamp abandoned his right ar before Blue was steady and he lurched away from t support. His third blow to Adderson's belly met fles ribs with a wild impact as the man turned away fro the attack. The unexpected force drove him to h knees, as Blue slammed sideways into the brok door.

There were voices. Full of anger, coming at hi Blue shook his head at the wonder of it and turn back to Adderson. The full force of the door caug him in the back, bowled him into his enemy, a brought them both to the softness of the manure-co ered ground.

He didn't hear the curses coming at him, did know the face of the small man that opened in su prise, or see him run back into the barn. Adderso face was what he could taste. He planted a fist on t offending nose and gloried in the bursting color of t red shower. The right hand was strong enough to ho onto the whisker-roughened neck. His left hand ca back repeatedly to dance across the shattered nos draw blood and flesh from the wide-angled hairine above the dark eyes.

He knew Adderson's knees came up in a furio attempt to stop him, could feel their impact at his bac and allowed a grunt to escape, but he was not turn from his slaughter of the man's face.

He did know the broom handle that slammed him om Adderson's body. Blue rolled with the force of e blow, felt a weightless freedom until he hit the torn uscles in his right arm. That pain slowed him and ened his mind to what was going on above him.

"He's mine, I got the dirty killing son of a bitch. That ty is mine."

Then a differing opinion offered in similar language. 'ou ain't got him. He's mine, this here's my barn and 's mine. Don't . . ."

There was a thud, and then heavy breathing. Blue as surprised to find it was his own breath. Then it arted again. Higher and wilder this time. More trants into the grab for the prize. Blue Mitchell. Blue anted to grin.

"That there killer belongs to me, got my gun on him w . . ."

"You be wanting the same slam to your head, can lige any time, he's mine. . . ."

There were more, all claiming him, none with much agination in their declaration. Blue wondered idly here Adderson had gone to, thought to roll his eyes en to look, but decided it wasn't worth the trouble.

Then things began to change.

"Chief, I got here first, knocked the bastard down, 's . . ."

"My stable, my hired man he's been walloping, he longs . . ."

'Look out you greedy so-and-so, I can take you any ne. This one's . . ."

Kind of funny, all these folks wanting him. Must l
what it's like to be popular. Blue guessed he'd as soo
be by himself. He finally opened his eyes.

There was a man standing over him, legs wide apa
sawed-off shotgun hanging at his side held with
strong hand. Kind of overkill, Blue figured. He wasn
going to fight anyone enough to need killing with su
a weapon. He grinned up at the man, who look
down with a puzzled face.

The clean face was familiar to Blue. He thought
it, then remembered. The man he'd asked directio
from earlier this morning. Seemed a long time ago.

Blue rolled his head in the dirt, spitting at the dr
ness on his tongue, and discovered a metallic taste
something warm sliding down his cheek into t
corner of his mouth. Damn, he was beginning to ha
the taste of blood. The voices continued their argui
over his head.

"Silence."

The word came in a roar accompanied by the sk
ward blast of the sawed-off shotgun. Blue gladly sh
his mouth and kept his words to himself. The rest
the swelling crowd reacted in the same way. The qui
was a blessed relief.

Blue looked for Bristol Adderson, rolling his he
from side to side. He finally found the man, flat out
his back, snoring with a flourish of bubbles throu
the flattened nose. Blue felt a pride in that reshapin
looked good on the sleeping man. He sighed deep
and found a deep bruised rib that objected. He final

ooked up, beyond the long legs of the man holding the moking shotgun.

Charlie Warner was there, a grin splitting his face ito whiskered halves. He was standing with the long-gged man, close enough to crawl in the pocket that eld the man's badge of office. Then there was the omber face of the girl. Celita. Black hair pulled into ild drawn braids, freckles strong against the paleness f her skin.

Blue smiled at her and tried to sit up. His right arm ouldn't take him and he lay back in the dirt. The nile let more blood into his mouth, and he coughed it the bitter taste, but kept the grin.

"You know, today is my birthday."

Celita couldn't help but return his grin. The puzzle-ent on the law's face was payment enough for the nsense words.

Blue set himself once more against the threatened otest of bruised muscle and stood, to balance on despread legs. He took one step forward. Celita fol-wed, fingers digging into his flesh as she struggled match his stride. The grin on Blue's bony face dened; it was all his now.

Center Point Publishing
600 Brooks Road • PO Box 1
Thorndike ME 04986-0001 USA

(207) 568-3717

US & Canada:
1 800 929-9108
www.centerpointlargeprint.com